The Gift
Coming of Age in Beringia

h.c. Clarke

Version: BGL

Nauja Books

Novels of American History
for Young People

"America was built on courage, on imagination and an
unbeatable determination to do the job at hand."

Harry S. Truman

Nauja Books
Medford, Oregon
http://naujabooks.com
h.c.clarke@naujabooks.com

Cover design: Haviland Hage

ISBN: 978-1-7346954-5-8

Disclaimer

- This is a work of fiction. Names, characters, places, events, locales, and incidents are either the products of the author's imagination or used in a fictitious manner. Any resemblance to actual persons, living or dead, or actual events is purely coincidental.

- This book is not intended as a substitute for the medical advice of physicians. The reader should regularly consult a physician in matters relating to his/her health and particularly with respect to any symptoms that may require diagnosis or medical attention.

- Although many of the scenes are based on evidence from actual archeological finds, they are by no means actual events or happenings, only possible (and fictional) events.

- Cultural philosophies are strictly the imagination of the author and do not represent any of the Native American or First Nations philosophies. Any resemblance is strictly coincidental.

- There have been many counting and weight systems used throughout history. Nauja not having counting words past four is fictional.

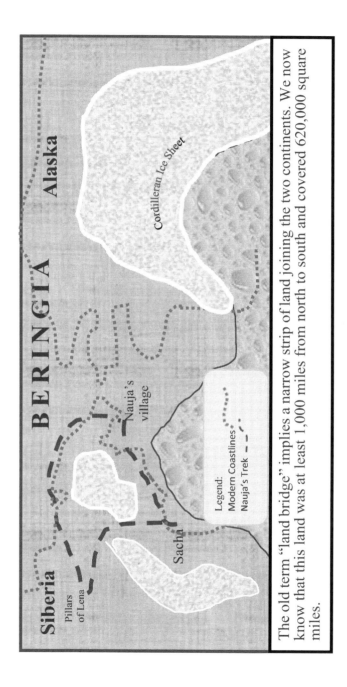

Siberia

Pillars
of Lena

BERINGIA

Alaska

Nauja's
village

Sacha

Cordilleran Ice Sheet

Legend:
Modern Coastlines
Nauja's Trek

The old term "land bridge" implies a narrow strip of land joining the two continents. We now know that this land was at least 1,000 miles from north to south and covered 620,000 square miles.

Measuring

Measuring distance without tools
Avg. ice age man—5'2" Modern man—6'

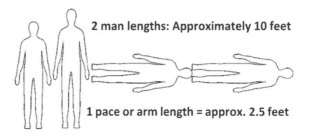

2 man lengths: Approximately 10 feet

1 pace or arm length = approx. 2.5 feet

Measuring time without tools

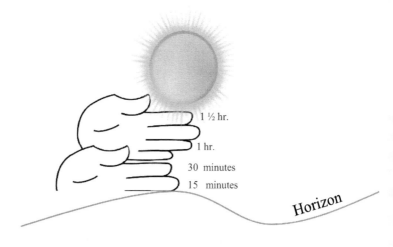

1 ½ hr.

1 hr.

30 minutes

15 minutes

Horizon

Counting

Counting with numbers

Nauja never uses counting words past four. Once at five, he says "one hand." For 6-9, he uses "one hand plus 1" or 2 etc. At 10, he simply says "both hands" or "both hands plus three" for 13." Some systems start counting knuckles or toes after reaching 10.

Counting Age by Life Stage

In prehistoric cultures, years were most likely unknown. Age was irrelevant and determined by seasons and these were not counted exactly. In this story, the people only count two seasons, dark-moons (winter) and light-moons (summer.) A child's skill level was more important than the number of seasons he or she had been alive. Children were placed in an age group according to their abilities to perform everyday tasks. The life span of these ancients was approximately 30-45 years.

Years	Life Stage	
0-4	Infant/toddler	
4-11	Childhood and Training Seasons	
	Boys: spear throwing, hunting, tool knapping,	**Girls:** gathering, cooking, sewing, preparing hides
12	Trek Preparation	Marriage
13-14	Trek Seasons	
15-22	Manhood Seasons	Child rearing
23-28	Middle Age	
28-	Old Age	

Counting Time

Prehistoric peoples may not have known about the cycle the earth takes to rotate around the sun. The obvious cycles are of the moon. Native Americans used nature to name the moons, although the nations differ in the names they assign.

Moons

Moon when ...

May	...rivers flow	Nov	...ground freezes
Jun	...berries ripen	Dec	1st ...with no light
Jul	...the tundra blooms	Jan	2nd...with no light
Aug	...all things ripen	Feb	...hunger comes
Sep	...geese leave	Mar	...bears waken
Oct	...hunting is best	Apr	...geese return

PREFACE

No one knows exactly how humans came onto the North American continent. They could have come through the corridor between the Laurentide and the Cordilleran ice sheet, which covered much of western Canada, as well as northern Washington, Idaho, and Montana. They could have taken boats along the Pacific coastline, or they could have come directly across the Pacific Ocean from southeast Asia, island by island. The only thing we know is that they came from somewhere else. No early hominid has been found in either of the American continents. Dinosaurs roamed across the Americas, and huge pterodactyls flew through their skies. The megafauna of the Pleistocene era included mammoths, mastodons, woolly rhinos, great bison and giant beavers. Horses and camels actually originated in the Americas.

But people came from somewhere else.

It took only 1,000 years to achieve the populating of the Americas. We know how long it took, but not how it began. Three competing theories continue to be researched, and each has good evidence to support it. There is still a lot of work to do. More archaeologists and anthropologists, linguists, and DNA specialists are needed. More data, data collectors, x-ray technicians, lab technicians, personnel support specialists and more fund raisers for all of the above are required.

The National Park Service website states:

> This area provides an unparalleled opportunity for a comprehensive study of the earth and human history. Its unusually intact landforms and biological and cultural remains may reveal the character of past climates and histories and the ebb and flow of earth's forces at the continents' edge. As one of the world's great ancient crossroads, Beringia may hold solutions to puzzles about who were the first people to populate North America, where and how they lived, how and when they traveled, and how they survived under such harsh climatic conditions.

This is the story of 13-year-old Nauja and why he and his people ventured onto the North American Continent. His world was a constant battle; giant bears and cats with dagger-like teeth were around every bend. We would think it a fantasy world if we didn't have proof of its existence. As you read, you will find interesting archeological, geographical, and geological information in the footnotes. You might also see clues to how I wrote the book.

If you find this story intriguing, consider preparing yourself to help solve the mysteries of the first immigration to the American continents.

Chapter 1
The Challenge
The value of a man resides in what he gives.

Nauja heard the howls of the lead wolf, calling for the pack to come together. He knew there wasn't much time. The small caribou had given up trying to stand on her broken leg. As he ran toward her, Nauja thanked the animal for her meat, skin, and bones. He knew he would not have time for a ritual. He ended her life quickly and started cutting the skin from her body.

The pack of large, strong wolves had assembled now. He could tell from their howls. The skinning was not perfect. Without other tribe members to keep the wolves away, acquiring the skin at all was enough.

He tossed the skin on the ground. Then he cut off a leg and threw it on the skin. He also wanted the head for its antlers and brain. He could make many tools from the antlers, and he needed the brain to cure the hide.

He could hear the snarls of the pack right behind him. The wolves were warning him to leave the kill. The wolves wouldn't want to fight him unless he tried to prevent them from taking the meat they needed.

He reached into the open belly. He grabbed a handful of the animal's insides and threw them as far away as he could. He just needed a tiny bit more time. He tossed the head onto the skin and headed away. He hoped the pack wouldn't think he was part of the kill.

~ ~ ~ ~ ~ ~

Siberia and Alaska are separated by 50 miles of water called the Bering Strait. During the last ice age, called LGM, the great ice sheets, or glaciers, sucked up the water. The land that was exposed is called Beringia. It was a vast steppe-tundra; a grassy world without any trees. A great wall of ice rising 1200 feet could be seen to the east.

Nauja's people thought the great ice sheet marked the end of the world. They thought the mammoth, camel, and other animals were born from the ice sheet. Then those animals returned there to die.

The people could not see the top of the great ice wall. Great storms of volcanic ash defined the area and kept it from view most of the time. When the storms calmed, there it was in the distant east. It was as if it were warning the people, "Do not come near, do not approach, this is the end of the world."

The sun had not yet fully risen. The young men, essentially boys, stood facing their chief. Nauja was standing at the end of a line of boys facing the chief. It was the last sun of the Moon When Geese Return. This sun is what they had spent their Preparation Seasons training for. Their manhood trek was about to begin.

The boys listened carefully. They had heard these words when the whole tribe gathered for the ceremony before. But now the words were spoken to them, so the words felt more important.

Old Átenaq, the chief, spoke. "You have now reached your first Trek Season. In four seasons you will be men. It is a great burden we place on you—to earn your right to live among us. Your challenge, your duty is to find a gift for the tribe. This gift must be useful items, knowledge, or technology. It must be something we do not yet know about."

"Go out into the world," continued the old chief. "You will be equipped with only your spears and your life-packs. You must travel alone for two moons. This will require you to hunt to feed yourself. If you cannot feed yourself, you will not be able to help feed the tribe. If you cannot help feed the tribe, we do not want you back.

"*If* you return, your status in the tribe will be according to

h.c. Clarke

the impact of your gift. This means that you may raise your station by your own efforts. The two with the best gift will become my advisors. If you are lazy and do not hunt for something truly new, your status will fall.

If you are the oldest son, when you return, you will become the head of your family. This means that your parents will enter their Middle Life seasons. Your younger brothers will become subject to your authority until they complete their own treks, and your sisters until they are mated. Lastly, if you are ready, you may ask for the mate of your choice."

Then Old Átenaq stood in front of each boy one by one. He laid his bent old hands on their upper arms. He leaned in, virtually touching foreheads. This way other boys nearby could not listen. He wanted to converse only with the boy in front of him. Nauja's best friend, Raven, was first in line, because he was Grandson-of-Chief. Nauja was at the end of the line because he was the only son of lowly parents.

Nauja was not the tallest boy, nor was he the shortest. He didn't have large muscles like Raven. He was lean but strong. Nauja didn't like to show off his skills the way the other boys did. Some of his abilities were not even seen as skills. His parents had taught him to do the work of everyone in the community, even incorporating the labor of women into his own skill set. He had to understand what it took to do each job.

His father had told him, "If you understand the work of other people, that work becomes more important to you. And you can choose your own work more wisely. All work should be respected. Even the most basic work would be missed if there were no one to do it."

Finally, Old Átenaq came to stand in front of Nauja. He put his hands on Nauja's shoulders and spoke softly. He looked directly at Nauja. "Go, my son. I expect great things of you. You are strong, stronger in body and mind than my own grandson.

Sometimes I wish you were my grandson.

"No, do not look surprised," continued the old leader. "I am not blind—yet. I have seen your strength. Raven is competent but at times he can be too proud or jealous. When this happens, he behaves unwisely. I know he has been your friend, justifying your behavior. He has defended you against the other boys when they bullied you. But did you ever notice when he stepped in? You, Nauja the Seagull, you are wise beyond your age."

Nauja did not feel comfortable with Chief Átenaq's words. He turned his eyes to look at the ground. The leader kept on. "Nauja, look at me. This is important." The chief waited until Nauja's eyes returned to his. "Raven is like his name. Ravens get other animals to do the work. Then they steal what they want. They have long memories and hold grudges. And, Nauja, Ravens will attack the nests of sea going birds.

But you, Nauja, you are like your name too. Seagulls[i] are just as smart as ravens. They are strategic but do not trick others. They do not hold grudges. They are good mates, and good parents. They are patient, tough and practical. "They know when to come together for the common good.

All these things I see in you, young Nauja of Beringia. I think you will bring your parents and me great pride. Go with these words. Find your way and bring yourself and your gift back to the People of Beringia that we may gain from your life."

Nauja was ready. He had packed his fire rocks, obsidian cutting stone, and a needle his mother had made from the bone of a pheasant. What room remained in his life-pack was stuffed with dried meat. A small bladder[ii] of water mixed with honey and ginger hung from his waist. He flexed his shoulders, shook his arms, and slowed his breathing. Yes, he was ready.

---

[i] Eskimo-Aleut, gull.

[ii] Native Americans historically dried and inflated bison bladders for use as containers.

4   h.c. Clarke

Chapter 2
The Trek Begins
Lessons come from the journey, not from the arrival.

Nauja started at a slow trot. He was excited yet fearful. His journey was across the vast steppe-tundra of Beringia. The moist ground was covered with the tiny dwarf willow and sage. The steppe-tundra lay before him as far as he could see. Small slopes rose and fell, rose and fell. When he looked up, he could see the top of the great ice mountain to the west. When he reached that point, he would have to turn south.

He reached behind his head and pulled off the thong binding his thick black hair. He focused on the beat of his movements rather than the parts of his body. Each strike of his foot on the soft steppe soil was the beat of a drum. Each breath was the sound of a rattle, and each whoosh of his hair the sound of a shaman's flute. Soon he reached a state where he would not become tired.

Part of Nauja's brain remained aware of the world. Knowing what is going on around you, can mean life or death. Once in a while he spotted herds of big game off in the distance. Nauja knew he would not be able to kill one by himself. Mammoth, wooly rhinoceros, and steppe-bison needed a large group of hunters to kill.

He focused on the small mammals. Normally, he wouldn't have bothered with them. His people only hunted them during starving times. They were also good for lining boots or hoods. They were also used for mittens.

As he trotted, he thought about the ceremony. Even though I was the last in line, did Old Átenaq think I was the best? Nauja wondered. I cannot let him down. I will look for a genuine contribution. I will look for knowledge which will make all our lives easier. But what possible item can I bring to the tribe? The tribe is old. No one remembers when they came to this land.

How can there still be something new, something unknown?

The cries of gulls, geese, and ducks pulled Nauja out of his thoughts and back to the world around him. He had gone too far into his thoughts. He often looked down to check for the signs of animals. The last thing Nauja wanted was to meet a spear-toothed cat with its long fangs that could rip out a man's throat. Nor did he want to meet a wolf, or a short-faced bear. The short-faced bear was as tall as a man even when it was walking on all fours. It had an arm span of three man-lengths.[i]

There were not many short-faced bears left. Older members of the tribe told of seeing one feeding on a dead mammoth. Its teeth dripped with rotting flesh. Old Átenaq told a story about this huge beast. It had chased the hunters away from their own kill. It didn't attack. Just its size was enough to make them give up their kill.

When twilight came[ii] and he was no longer able to go around the damp areas, Nauja looked for a dip in the ground. It just needed to be big enough to keep him from the wind. His tunic and a fire would keep him warm.

His tunic was a large hide with a hole in the middle. Cuts were made under each arm. The ends were sewed together using an awl to make holes and sinew as thread. The rest of the hide was wrapped around his waist and securing it with a belt. It fell to the middle of his thighs. It would get shorter when he cut strips off the bottom to use for one thing or another.

He hung the sheep's bladder full of water and life-pack from the belt. He would hang other tools from his belt as he made them. During the sun, he wore it fur side out. At dark he turned the fur side in for greater warmth.

As he made his way, he picked up any sticks in his path.

---

[i] Arctodus simus is considered to be one of the largest known terrestrial mammalian carnivores that has ever existed.
[ii] Twilight is its own opposite. Sunset/sunrise, dusk/dawn, twilight/twilight.

h.c. Clarke

He tied them together with a piece of hide. Then he slung them over his shoulder. He also looked for bones or piles of dung he came across, anything that would burn. There were no large trees on the steppe-tundra. His people had learned to burn whatever they could find that would give off heat or light. There were signs that there had once been spruce. Now they were only in the songs and stories of the elders.

Most of the boys did not stay alone until their Preparation Seasons. Nauja's father had made him spend the night alone when he had been in his last Childhood Season. He had started everything earlier than the other boys. Raven had not stayed alone until just before his trek.

Nauja's father made him start everything earlier than the other boys. His father had told him, "I was so afraid those first nights. I was not ready for the loneliness on my own trek. You must be prepared." Nauja had been very afraid that first time. He had crouched under a small tent made from an antelope skin over a tripod in front of a fire. His dinner was dried meat strips. He had spent most of the night silently crying. He cursed his mother who made him work so hard and his father for making him stay alone so young.

Near dawn, he had fallen asleep. But it had been a fitful sleep. And he had dreamed. He had dreamed of the stars his father had made him study. His father had pointed out Star-That Does-Not-Move.

"That one," his father said. "It will be your guide. Each sunrise check it before you start out. It must be on your right until you come to the great ice mountain. Then keep it to your back. Never forget to check it each morning. If you forget, you may walk a sun for nothing."

In his dream the Star-That-Does-Not-Move had fallen out of the sky. Nauja saw it fall. As it fell it turned bright blue. As blue as the sunlight sky between storms. It had shone brighter than he'd ever seen it shine before. In his dream, it had fallen right on him. Then it went into his heart, a tiny sparkling blue flame. Then it had bounced off his chest and flown right back to the sky. When he woke up, he had looked at his chest, and he had a burn right where the star had landed.

When he told his mother about the blue star and showed

her the burn over his heart, she had just stared at him. Then she backed away, fear on her face. She realized she had to protect this only child of hers. She bent her head close so no one could watch her mouth even though no one was around to look.

"This dream, on your very first night alone, is a sign," she had whispered. "That star wants you to know it in your heart. That is why it left you with a mark. Never tell anyone about your dream. Never. They will be afraid. People are unpredictable when they are afraid. Tell the others an ember from the fire popped onto your chest."

"Why was it as blue as the sky between storms?" he had asked. "It was the color of snow under snow when Father took me to see the ice mountain. Shimmery blue."

"That too is a sign. When you are old enough for your manhood trek, you must look for blue. It is a rare color. Even flowers hardly ever come in blue. The star wants you to find blue, so look for it carefully. It will guide you. It will watch over you. But NEVER tell anyone about the blue star."

As the nights, isolated and alone, went from one to two to four and more, Nauja started to doubt that he could go on a trek by himself. "Father, I was so lonely. The only thing that made it bearable was knowing that I would be coming home to you and Mother. A manhood trek is not just one or two suns. It is one, or even two sun *cycles*. What if I can't make the trek by myself?"

"Don't worry my little Seagull," Mother had replied. "You are still young and there is still time to train. When you feel like you are going uphill, tell yourself you will make it. If you think you can, you will be able to."

Now, thoughts of his parents were the predominant reason for his loneliness. He ached with loneliness. He had spent many nights alone in training for his trek. But then he had known that a warm meal and a hug waited for him in just a few suns. The only thing he could look forward to now was a sun filled with danger and a night filled with fear.

h.c. Clarke

Chapter 3
Survival

Respect all that is part of the great circle of life.

Nauja thought about all this on the first night of his trek. On the second night he stared up at the stars. His tribe believed that each star was the soul of an ancestor watching over their many times over grandchildren below.

How long has my tribe been around if each star was a soul of an ancestor. Will the stars change when I leave my tribe's lands? Will I see new stars? Perhaps the stars of another tribe's ancestors?

He decided to watch the stars each evening so that he could tell when he left his tribe's lands. The stars should change.

On the fourth night, the stars still had not changed. How can that be? he speculated. Surely after four nights I have left our lands. There is my blue star, the Star-That-Does-Not-Move.[i] How could Father have told me always to check the star-that-does-not-move if he thought the stars would change. Maybe there are no tribes when you walk with the wind? Maybe there is just one tribe in the sky.

Whenever Nauja noticed signs of other tribes, he avoided them. He was afraid of meeting strange people. Not all of them were friendly. After half a moon, his survival became mental as well as physical. The loneliness became awful. Even with a fire close, he felt a cold deep in his heart. The kind of cold no fire could make warm. The impact of his loneliness was a numbness, an emptiness inside. He no longer cared about the world around him. He even welcomed a quick death from a fierce animal. At

---

[i] Polaris, the current North Star, does move but, its circle is so small it looks as if it doesn't. Because the Earth's axis wobbles, our perception of north gradually shifts to other stars over a 26,000-year cycle. Vega was the North Star at the time of this story and will regain that status in about 12,000 years.

times he couldn't differentiate between what was real and unreal.

One night the green northern lights were swirling faster and brighter than Nauja had ever seen them. Swirls of both red and yellow moved into the green ones. From the yellow, he saw two moons drip down. They hung there in front of him just beyond his fire. Then there were four moons, then six and eight. The moons started to cry. They moaned and shrieked. Bloody tears dripped from their eyes.

The next morning, he saw wolf tracks. They were not moons but the glowing eyes of a wolf pack waiting to attack in case my fire died down, he thought. He remembered what his mother had said, "If you get so lonely you feel you cannot go on, talk to your star." So, he started talking to his blue star. Watch over me, Blue Star. Keep me company, keep me safe, keep my fire burning.

At the beginning of each sun, he talked to his star. "Where do you go in the light, Blue Star? If you don't move in the dark, do you run to catch up in the light? Maybe you are the chief of the souls. Why did you talk to me when I had a hand plus three sun cycles? And why did Old Átenaq say he wished I were his grandson? Have you talked to Old Átenaq? Did you tell him to say that to me?" he said out loud since no one was about to call him crazy-boy-who-talks-to-himself.

Just for fun, he'd throw his spear at a hare or ground squirrel not even attempting accuracy. As it ran away unhurt, he'd talk to it. "Don't think I couldn't have killed you if I wanted. I'm glad you got away. Your puny little hides won't add to my status at all. The dark moons have just ended. You are skinny and not worth killing."

After the complete moon cycle, Nauja noticed huge paw prints. Huge paw prints followed by other smaller prints. A bear! And her cubs! He amended his direction. He didn't want to meet a bear. Any animal with babies is dangerous. Normally, a bear would ignore a man unless it felt threatened.

A bear with cubs would assume Nauja was a danger to her family and simply attack.

Despite his attempt to avoid the bear family, as he came to the top of a rise in the ground, Nauja stood face to face with the mother and her two cubs. They were not more than a stone's throw away. It was a short-faced bear!

No, I am wrong. The elders said short-faced bears are taller on four legs than a man on two. This one is not taller than I am. But she looks scary enough, and with cubs, she will assume I am a threat.

He debated his choices. He could act assertive in hopes that she would take her cubs and leave, but he didn't think she would do that. He decided to back away slowly and hope she had not noticed him. He knew he had to remain down wind of her. He stood still, trying to determine where she was going.

After a few moments, the she-bear and her cubs hadn't moved at all. *She's probably found or made a kill. That will make her even more dangerous if she sees me. The smart thing to do is to go back the way I came.*

The she-bear looked up. She moved her snout in the wind until her gaze settled on Nauja. He stood very still. The sow slapped her huge paw on the ground. This was her way of telling Nauja to go away. Nauja thought about the old stories. He hoped they had not been exaggerating. He backed off slowly. He kept his eyes on the mother bear but never straight into the eyes of the sow.

"I am sorry great mother," he articulated clearly in a gentle voice. "I did not mean to stop your dinner. I will leave you and your beautiful family." Slowly he backed away. The she-bear let out a loud huff and started walking toward him. *This is not good. A mother bear would not leave her cubs unless she felt they were in danger. She is going to chase me!*

As soon as he couldn't see her anymore, he turned and ran as fast as he could. He went down the hill in leaps and bounds. He hoped only that he did not fall. He could both hear and feel the pounding of her great paws on the ground behind him.

Zig zagging may throw her off and make her give up, but ALL bears can easily outrun a man, he thought.

Making one last attempt at talking her out of attacking, Nauja stopped and turned to face the bear. To make himself look bigger, he waved his arms above his head. He yelled at the top of his lungs, "Go away you big, smelly-mouthed lunk. Go back to your stupid looking cubs. You better go back before a cave lion gets those babies. In fact, I think I smell fire. Run back to your home, your house is on fire, your children will burn."

Yelling didn't work either.

The bear did stop…for a second. She shook her head back and forth. Opening her great mouth wide, she chuffed and grunted and then clacked her teeth together. Nauja could virtually feel the slashing of her claws, shredding the skin on his back.

I will not feel the pain for long. As soon as I am down, she will sever my neck with one bite. Father, I am sorry. I have let you down. You will never know what happened to me. Oh, Blue Star if you are watching over me as Mother said you would be, now is the time to give me help.

Chapter 4
Discovering Blue
May the stars carry your sadness away.

Out of nowhere a huge black cloud let loose its fury. Hail, the thickness of two fingers, blasted down upon the tundra. Nauja had never seen hail before. He had never seen rain. The only storms in his life were the great winds, consisting of ash and sand or both. He was so shocked that he couldn't move. Then he realized that whatever was hitting him, hurt. He covered his head with his arms. Then he found a set of moose antlers lying on the ground. He put the two close together and sat on his heals underneath them. He pulled his tunic over his head. When the storm passed, Nauja couldn't help thinking that it was his star that had saved his life.

Well, Blue Star, are you testing me? Be careful what I ask for, is that what you are telling me? These balls of ice saved my life. But they might have killed me if I had not found the antlers.

He didn't see any signs of the bear, but he couldn't resist going back to the top of the rise where it had been. There was no trace that the bear or her cubs had ever been there. What he did find was a bee buzzing where the bear and her cubs had been feasting. *A bee! A bee means honey. No one passes up the opportunity to follow a bee*, he thought.

The she-bear had downed a bee tree. Despite the ice storm, the bees were still buzzing around the dead tree. They were busily building the nest again. It looked like there was plenty of honey still there. Nauja quickly built a small fire as close to the log as possible without scaring the bees. When the fire was going strong, he added damp sage to make it smoke. He took one large burning stick from the fire. He waved it back and forth as he approached the bee tree.

Most of the bees flew away, leaving a few to guard the nest. Nauja braced himself for the stings and ran into the smoke. He used his cutting stone to scoop the honey and the comb into a pouch. He had made the pouch from a section of his own tunic while waiting for the fire to smoke. When the pouch was full, he ran away from the tree.

When he was far enough away, he took off his clothes and slapped the remaining bees. He shook his clothes and boots to free them of the last bees.

Then he scraped at each of the stings with his cutting stone to remove the stingers. He wished he could dip himself in a creek or river, but none was around. He looked around and found a small pile of the ice rain that had not melted. He rubbed the semi-melted ice over his body. Then he wiped a bit of the honey from the pouch over each sting. Finally, he put his clothes back on.

But just in case, he picked the bark off the tiny tundra willow stems and chewed it. This would help with any fever he might get from the stings.[i] It may even preclude one from starting. He was happy with the thought of the honey in the pouch.

The next sun, Nauja realized that his dried meat was almost gone. Now he'd have to catch a hare or squirrel, or maybe a ptarmigan. They wouldn't be very fat. But at least they would be hot and easier to chew than his dried meat. It would take a sun or two catch these clever animals. Nauja watched his supply of dried meat carefully.

This must be the reason Old Átenaq allows us two suns at occasional stopping points, he thought.

Well before dark, Nauja searched the ground for signs of the small animals. He looked for tiny paths to the shallows of a small creek. He looked for broken willow stems and slightly moved leaves. He wanted proof that his snare would trap an animal. He was sure that he would make a kill because he had seen the scat of varied animals.

He braided several long strings of sinew. These were the long tendons of animals that connect bone to bone or bone to muscle. This made a strong rope. One which a hare would not be able to chew. Next, he looped the sinew around itself and tied it off loosely. This would allow him to pull the snare quickly, tightening it around a hare's leg. Then he would rush in and slit the hare's throat. *I will cause it as little pain as I can. I will thank it for its life*

---

[i] Honey has antibacterial properties, and willow contains salicylic acid, the precursor of aspirin.

h.c. Clarke

that I may sustain my own, he thought.

He placed a bit of dried meat just past the large loop. This way the hare, he hoped, would stop to nibble on the meat and Nauja would pull it tight. He rolled in the tundra sage to mask his own smell and lay down on his stomach to wait.

Falling asleep is the biggest danger in snaring an animal, Nauja thought. *If I fall asleep, I will miss the hare's stop to inspect the meat. If that happens, I will lose not only the hare but the bait as well.*

He lay still and waited. Twilight came. The air started to cool. *If I keep my thoughts on a nice fire with a hare roasting on a spit, I might trick my brain into thinking I am warm and safe even though I am cold and hungry.* His muscles ached from being so still. He was in danger from larger beasts coming to the creek to drink or to catch a hare of their own.

Finally, the moment came. He felt the animal more than saw it. Patience was the key. He couldn't pull too soon or too late. If he did, he would not get a strong hold on the hare and he would go hungry another sun. But like a cat, he had learned patience.

He squinted into the evening dusk. He looked for a small shadow blocking the tundra plants. Nauja jerked hard on the length of braid. He was rewarded with the short squeal of a trapped animal. An hour later his vision was a reality. Nauja sat before a warm fire, a skewered hare dripping fat that fed the flames.

Nauja stayed by the creek the following sun. He snared several small animals. He soaked each of the skins overnight in the creek. Then he scraped every bit of meat and muscle from the leather side. Finally, he smoked them over his fire.

He used the internal organs as bait. The hare skins would make soft, warm linings for mittens and boots or a hood for the following dark moons. And they were not bulky to carry. He simply tucked them into his tunic belt.

He sliced strips of the meat. Then laid half of them out in the sun on the grass to dry. He covered these strips with a light layer of sage. This would help keep sand and dirt from settling on them as well as give them a wonderful flavor. Other pieces he hung above his fire to smoke.

Two suns later, his life-pack was full with meat and his body rested. He still travelled lightly. This way he could go far each sun. As Nauja left the steppe and entered the tundra, he slowed his trot as his father had told him.

"The tundra is arid. It will drink the sweat from your body. Sweating will cause your body to get colder. It is always the cold that is the enemy," his father had warned.

Each sun, Nauja entered the state where he became unaware of his body. His thoughts kept him company. They chased away the loneliness of the previous night. He often thought about his mother.

My mother is crazy-woman. Woman-who-cannot-keep-a-child-alive. The other women in the tribe ignore her. I know she is not crazy. She is Mother. She is tough. She is strong-willed. She is strong minded. I am healthy because of her. I am skilled because of her. I am alive because of her.

Two of the sons that had come before Nauja walked the wind after only two moons. And another son and daughter had been born together. They had already walked the wind before their birth.

Mother still talks to my siblings. I've heard her in quiet times. She says they told her to name me Nauja because seagulls are adaptable; seagulls not only survive but thrive everywhere. She says it is my duty to my siblings to live their lives for them. I must have five times the strength of the other boys of the tribe, five times the speed, five times the knowledge.

Nauja's thoughts would also turn to Yuka. *I am not too worried that another boy will choose her before me. The others do not like her. I only hope she will accept me when I choose. Should I speak to her before the ceremony? She is so much like Mother. But what if my gift does not bring me status? Maybe she will not want to marry a man with a low status, and she shouldn't. She deserves more.*

The part of his brain that was always aware of the world around him brought him out of his reverie. He heard the faint

h.c. Clarke

cry of the caribou, already close to death from her broken leg. He also heard the howls of the wolves. He knew there wasn't much time. He would have to kill it quickly or he would become part of the meal.

There wasn't enough time to do a good job. He skinned the animal as best he could. He tossed the skin on the ground near him. He hastily cut a leg bone for meat and threw it on the skin. He needed the head for the brains and horns. The howls had changed to threatening snarls. He knew they were close behind him.

The wolves didn't want to fight him. They would if he tried to prevent them from taking the meat. He reached into the belly and grabbed a handful of the steaming entrails. He threw them as far away as he could. The wolves set upon them fighting with each other over the first meal they'd had in many suns.

Hopefully those will satisfy them for just a few moments more, thought Nauja. He sliced through the rest of the neck and tossed the head onto the skin.

He grabbed the skin and left. As he left the bloody scene, he happened to notice a small she-wolf hanging back from the rest of the pack. She looked different from the others. She was smaller size. She also had large patches of white fur.

Nauja turned away from her. He hoped she would not warn the pack of his retreat. They might think he was stealing their meat. He wanted to get as far away from the horde as he could.

He needed a safe place to process the skin and smoke the meat. But he turned one last time to look at the strange she-wolf. She turned to look at him also. Their eyes met. She had one blue eye! It was the color of the sky between storms. It was the color of snow under snow! And it glinted at him.

His blue star shone in her eye. In that short look, their souls touched. It was almost in recognition of a shared life. Upset, Nauja turned back to the tundra ahead and trotted forward. He wanted to get away from the look of the she-wolf and her blue-starred eye.

It was late after high-sun. Twilight would not arrive for many hands of the sun. Having reached the great ice-covered mountains, he looked for a small cave. A place where the caribou's skin could block out the night wind and chill. Twice he noticed large caves, but a cave lion or bear might be living in them.

Many times, cave lions entered the dens of bears. It was an easy kill while the bears were hibernating. But it was too late in the season for that. Meeting the mother bear and her cubs at the bee tree proved that. But he still worried about any large cave.

Besides, these caves are too close to the wolf pack. I want to get farther away. What if the pack is large? The small caribou might not be enough to feed all of them. Then they might follow me.

I can prevent the meat smell from creating a path straight to me, he thought. He took the time to slice a strip of the hide. He rolled the skin into a loose roll and tied it with the strip. He lifted the bundle over a shoulder, trotting off as fast as he could, to make up for lost time.

As he hurried away, another thought entered his mind—the touching of souls with the strange she-wolf. It still disturbed him. Was it just the unusual glint in her eye, or the fact that one, and only one, of her eyes was blue? It was the color of his dream star. His mother's words came back to him, "It is a sign. When you are old enough for your manhood trek, you must look for the rare blue."

Is the color important? Should I go back?

h.c. Clarke

Chapter 5
The Animal
We can judge the heart of a man by his treatment of animals.

Her mother and siblings had been killed. She was the brave one. She had been exploring away from the den when the lion had attacked. Now, all alone, she had been following this pack for several moons. She was trying to keep herself alive on the cleaned bones they left behind. It had been many suns since the group had found or made a kill large enough to feed the entire pack.

Only a few were strong and healthy. Many were hungry. A few were starving. She was one of those. When the leader of the pack called the others, she hoped the kill would be big enough that she would be allowed to have a bone from it. She had learned to keep away from the others and be thankful for the leftovers they allowed her to have.

When they approached the caribou, an animal she had never seen before was already there. The animal was ripping it apart, but it wasn't eating any of it. It was a very strange being. Its fur fell loose on its body. It looked like it wasn't really attached. And its legs had hardly any fur at all. Yet the fur from its head looked completely different. It fell long and loose like a horse's mane.

It sat without sitting. It sat on just its back paws. It looked like it was relieving itself. As they came near, the animal with the long mane used its front paws to toss the pack the insides of the caribou. Then it stood upright on its back paws like a bear. It used its front paws to drag the caribou's skin. The skin was loaded with the head and one leg. It walked away hurriedly. She smelled fear around this strange animal.

As it left, it looked at her. Their gazes met, and she felt a shiver she'd never felt before. A thrill inside her. It had nothing to do with her hunger. It made her heart beat faster. She felt she was part of this animal. She felt that they had once been one, but she knew she had never seen anything like it before.

She must be closer to death than she had thought. Maybe the animal was near death too. She turned her attention back to the pack and the dead caribou. Hunger forced her to inch forward on her belly toward the kill.

She whined, attempting to gain pity from the leader. He answered her with a deep, nasty growl warning her to stay away. "Keep her away," he told the lesser wolves. "She is other, not of our pack, not of our kind." He would not bother with her, and would not let her eat, even if she were dying. She was nothing to him.

Five of the younger males turned on her. They went toward her slowly. They showed their teeth, dripping with the caribou's blood. She backed off. Her hunger might kill her but not as quickly as being torn apart by these five wanting to gain favor with the leader. She could easily become part of the feast instead of its feasters. That is the code of the wild.

She slunk away. She was not going to be allowed to eat any of the meat. The females and the younger males would be the final diners. They would crack the bones to lick out every trace of the rich marrow.

The other wolves didn't realize that there was another smell of caribou. It was mixed with a strange odor. This second smell was moving away from the dead caribou. It followed the path

h.c. Clarke

of the new animal that walked on two legs.

She followed the weaker scent. She tried to determine the other odor masking that of the caribou. She knew she would not last long. Her mother had not lived long enough to teach her how to catch the small rodents. She must have meat or die. She followed the scent away from the pack.

She was just about to give up. The blood smell of the caribou became stronger. It was mixed with the other animal smell. She followed. She crept slowly and carefully. She tried to blend into the brush as she inched forward on her belly.

Her need for food overcame her intense fear of the animal sitting in front of a small cave. It was no more than a hollow in the rock wall. It was the animal that had looked at her. The one that made her heart beat faster. He was again sitting without really sitting.

Despite his size, he didn't look scary. He had no claws, no fangs extending from his flat face. Did he have speed?

He did not seem to smell her. How could he with a flat nose attached to his face without a snout that sticks out? This animal must have other strong powers that she could not see.

He turned his head slowly this way and that. He used his tiny nose to sniff the wind. She had been wrong when she thought he had not detected her. But no low growl came from his throat. His lips didn't curl back to show sharp teeth.

He was in front of Fire yet was not afraid of it. What animal is not afraid of Fire? He seemed to control it. Had Fire felt the same thing she had felt? Had it felt as if it were part of the animal?

The caribou leg was suspended above Fire, its fat dripping. Fire flared in delight, waiting for the next drop of fat. But Fire never stopped for meat when it ran free on the tundra. It ran and ran and wanted more and more. But the fire didn't scare the strange animal. It remained docile. This creature must have other powers that she could not see.

She looked at the loose-furred animal with a long mane. Did it have speed? Did it have agility? Do I have the energy to rush in and steal the meat from Fire? The new animal reached for the caribou leg. He turned a stick to rotate the meat above fire. The leg teased fire with new fat to lick.

She now noticed the stick coming out of each end of the meat. The ends were resting on other sticks with a split at the top. They were stuck into the ground on each side of fire. Could she run in and grab the stick above Fire? Will Fire chase her as it chases all animals it finds? Maybe he will order Fire to attack her.

Her stomach made a grumbling noise. Figuring out this new animal would take more time than she had. The squatting animal turned to face her. She was sure he saw her. Now her life would end.

Nauja heard the crackle of woody plants. The sage he used on the meat had taken over his sense of smell. Every boy during their Preparation Seasons learned which of the animals could be eaten. His mother had taught him the plants that would make food better.

He had rubbed sage into the meat before placing it on its skewer. He pushed the stick back into the meat. He crushed sage into the hole before he put the stick in again. The meat began to cook, and the fat dripped into the fire.

The smell of meat and fat was making his mouth water. Then he heard the crackling of scrub birch. He pointed his nose in each direction. He tried to locate the musky wolf smell. *It is more subtle than it had been. Well, the fire should scare all but the bravest wolves away,* he thought. *And the smell would be stronger if there were many.*

Despite this thought, he continued to scan the air, trying to locate the creature. There! There it is. He noticed her because

h.c. Clarke

of the white patches on her fur which did not blend very well with the tundra plants. She was not more than a stone's throw away. He saw the bony female with the one blue eye he had noticed earlier.

She started to whimper. She was testing whether or not he would attack her. Nauja studied the animal. *She looks like a wolf but is a lot smaller. Even female wolves are not that small*, Nauja thought. He spoke in a quiet soothing voice, "I can see your ribs under your skin. You are obviously starving to death. Didn't the pack allow you to eat? You left it to follow me. Why? You are asking for food. Did your pack make you starve?"

Her fur would make a warm lining, and she would be easy to kill. She whimpered again, inching herself closer on her belly. As she came closer, Nauja could see that her fur was bare in places, not full and warm. "You won't live long. You will probably freeze tonight. I can just wait until you die," Nauja said in a gentle voice.

As he was studying her, their eyes met again. He felt her beating heart. The one blue eye stared intensely at him. The blue of the sky between storms. The blue of snow under snow. The blue of his star! It scared him. Again, he felt his soul touching another. It was a knowing.

His tribe knew how to help starving people. It was not uncommon to have starving times at the end of dark moons when food stores ran low. It couldn't be that different with animals. Without thinking what he was doing, he sliced a thin sliver of the meat off the skewer and threw it her way. She yelped in fear but was too weak to retreat.

She lay there staring at him. She looked him right in the eye. That soft glint he noticed before returned in the one blue eye. *A wolf would never look a man in the eye, which confirms that this creature was not truly a wolf,* thought Nauja.

She must have determined that he would not kill her. She gathered her final reserves and pulled herself toward the meat. She only nibbled at it, licking the fat off first.

After each bite, she looked up at him to see if he was going to spring out at her. When she had eaten only part of the piece he had thrown, she lay back, and closed her eyes.

Was she dead? Or was she sleeping after eating all her weak stomach could handle. He approached. She didn't stir. He picked up his drinking bladder and sat cross-legged at her back where she would have to turn to bite him. He didn't think she had that much energy. She didn't wake up. He dribbled just a bit of water onto the back of her snout, careful to make sure it dripped inside. Then a little more.

When she stirred, he backed off, but she didn't move again. He dribbled the water into her snout but moved the water bladder closer to get more between her lips than before. He got up to get more water from the spring.

When he came back, she was still lying down. She was looking at him closely. He came near her slowly. Her strange two-colored eyes tracked his movements.

He went to the fire, sliced off a bit more meat and laid it on a flat rock. He spoke aloud to her in a soft, gentle voice.

"You are too weak to eat the meat whole, wolf-animal. I will mash this meat for you. Now I will add fat drippings." He held the pounding rock beneath the caribou leg until it was covered with fat. The he blended this into the mashed meat on the flat rock. He added just a tiny bit of water and mixed it again.

"I will add ginger root to your water. Mother says it helps with stomach pains and wards off sickness. You are so skinny that your stomach may cause you pain."

He scraped the mash onto his cutting stone and came near the animal. "I know you do not have the energy to kill me, so I will try to help you eat." This time he sat down in front of her where she could keep her eyes on him.

He took a stick and scraped off the mash from his cutting stone. He approached the starving animal. He brought the stick to the front of her snout despite the low growl she managed to produce. When the stick was close enough, she licked off the mashed meat, keeping her eyes on his.

He spoke to her again, in a soothing voice, "You are such a curious animal. Why do you look me straight in the eye? You look at me as if you know what I am thinking. Did you feel our souls touching as I did? Is that why you let me come close? You know that I will not

24   h.c. Clarke

hurt you, but how do you understand this?

"And why do you have one blue eye? Are you blind in that eye like the elders who live longer than they should? But you are still very young, I can tell.

"That is enough for now. Starving stomachs must be carefully monitored. Eating too much too soon can kill faster than the starvation itself. Now you must have water. I know that animals drink with their tongues. I will try to make a bowl so you can drink."

He returned to the caribou skin and cut a small circle from the hide. He rubbed it back and forth with a rock, dislodging most of the meat and fat from the leathery side. He returned to the animal, forming a bowl by shaping it around his fist. He placed the leather bowl on the ground in front of her and poured the ginger water into it.

"Now, can I trust you? I know you are afraid. I am afraid too. You cannot kill me in your condition, but a deep bite would slow my journey. I don't understand why I am helping you, but I must find out how the blue star got into your eye. Did it touch you in a dream like me? I will show you the scar later. First you must drink."

He pushed the water bowl to her snout, ignoring the low rumble in her throat. Then he waited. She looked at the water and the hand that did not retract and then back into his eyes. Holding his gaze, she brought her tongue forward and licked out the water.

When he moved his other hand closer to fill the water, she growled weakly again. But she did not take her snout away. After he had poured more water into the bowl, she licked it dry and waited for more. He poured water into his bowl four more times.

Then she looked at him closely. The blue eye shimmered in the sun. Slowly she laid her head back on the ground and closed her eyes to sleep. Nauja could not take his own eyes off the sleeping eyes of this animal. This animal with the blue star eye.

"I've found the color blue, Mother," whispered Nauja. "And this blue is just like the blue star of my dream." *Why would my star come to me in the form of a wolf? Is this where the star-that-does-not-move goes during the sun? Into the eye of this animal? Tonight, I will look to see if it is gone from her eye.*

Would the knowledge of where the star-that-does-not-move goes during the sun be knowledge enough for the tribe? How would that knowledge help? No, this cannot be my gift. But maybe this animal can help me find my gift. Maybe the star went into the animal's eye, so it could help me find my gift.

Nauja took care of the wolf-like animal until twilight. Each time he held the stick a bit farther away from her. She had to inch her body closer to the fire. When she slept, Nauja worked on the caribou hide. He took the skin to the creek to soak overnight. He would have to scrape all the meat from the skin before tanning it with the animal's own brain.

When dark came, he lay down along the back of the animal. He knew she would not attack him. The fire was on one side and the animal on the other. They shared their body heat. The fire was now close enough to provide just enough added heat to keep them both from freezing.

h.c. Clarke

Chapter 6
Ktoh

**If you talk to the animals,
they will talk with you and you will know each other.**

When Nauja awoke at sunrise, the animal was sitting on her haunches staring down at him. He turned a bit and was rewarded with a throaty growl. But her lips did not pull back. The two of them, man and beast, locked their gazes. Each sized up the intentions of the other. Then the different-than-wolf animal walked around him. She leaned down and nudged the meat stick.

"Are you asking for more food? Why didn't you just take the skewered meat? The fire is cold and could not hurt you," he said in a voice he knew would not frighten her.

Slowly rising, he went to the fire, sliced off another piece of meat and tossed it to her whole this time. She gulped it down and studied him again. Then she ambled around the rock wall toward the spring. He waited. *Will she return, or will she continue on her own journey?*

Shortly, the animal came back with the caribou hide in her mouth. She dropped it in front of him as if to ask, "Did you lose this in the stream?"

Nauja was amazed. "You can hear my thoughts! I was just thinking I should get the skin from the creek and here you bring it to me. What are you?"

She sat on her haunches looking at him. Then she turned and focused on the cold meat over the coals and then back to him. She made a sound he had never heard. It was comparable to the furred sea animals in the ocean but was deeper and shorter in length.

Nauja chuckled. "You think you did me a favor and now you want more meat for your trouble? Members of my own tribe would not be as polite as you are. I guess you earned your breakfast. I do not have to get the hide myself. But I would have given you more meat anyway."

He gave her another slice of the cold meat and cut one for himself. They ate in friendly silence. His own hunger was satisfied, he took the leg bone and cut the rest of the meat from it.

"Well, whatever animal you are, I have a lot of work to do. Stay if you please, and I hope you do. I want to learn about you."

He rubbed a leg bone against a flat rock. He rubbed the leg sideways and back and forth along the edge of the rock. He wanted a slight edge. He placed the hide on his rock. He used sharpened bone to scrape off everything from the inside of the skin.

The wolf-like animal watched him in silence. He took the skin back to the spring. He stood on it while he washed himself, rubbing his body with sand from the edge of the spring. The wolf-like animal had followed him to the stream. She sat along the shore watching.

"You are studying me as much as I study you. I wish I knew what you thought of me." He rolled the hide tightly to keep in the moisture and tied it with a strip he had cut off the edge.

He packed up his cutting stone and wrapped the remaining meat in a small part of the skin. He returned to the spring one last time to fill his water bladder and hooked it securely into his waist thong. He grabbed his spear and motioned with his head. Then he started trotting west once more. He did not look back. When the sun was high in the sky and he became hungry, he looked to see if she had followed.

He squatted down near a dwarf birch and retrieved the saved meat. She was there. Turning to the wolf-animal, he spoke to her, "If you are going to go with me on my trek, you need a name. I will call you Ktoh, Who. I do not know what kind of animal you are.

"Why did you leave your pack? Were you lonely? I know how it feels to be lonely despite being among people. Ktoh, here is your piece of meat. Try not to gulp it down; your stomach is still weak."

Ktoh seemed to understand as she licked the meat layer by layer until it was gone. She then pawed at the ground. She dug a small hole several fingers deep. She sat down in front of it and whimpered softly.

Nauja placed the hide bowl he had made into the hollow and poured water into it. He stepped back as soon as it was full. Ktoh lapped up the water eagerly. She looked up for more. He filled it again. She lapped up the quickly before it could soak through the now saturated hide.

"Ok, Ktoh, we'd better be on our way. I wonder if you will stay with me until I find my gift. Or are you just staying with me until you find a pack that will not make you lonely?

The pair resumed their trek. Ktoh followed. In the following suns she would run off on her own, but she always returned. When she came back, she always dropped a tundra hare in front of him.

The first time this happened, Nauja couldn't help but comment, "Thank you, Ktoh. You are a good hunter as well as a pleasant companion. I am glad you have chosen to come with me. I have never had such a good friend, other than Raven. All the other boys …well you are a good companion. Let's leave it at that. I hope you will stay with me. I don't feel so lonely when you are here.

"I just wish you could talk to me. Feel free to participate in our conversation if you have anything to add. I would especially like to know about you. What kind of animal are you? Where did you come from? Why were you with that wolf pack? Are you a wolf, or something else? See how many questions I have, Ktoh. And I wonder if Yuka would approve of you. If you choose to stay with me, it will be important that she approve of you."

"Woof," Ktoh replied.

"And why do you not return to the pack? I saw you

hanging back from it. Were they bullying you because you are different? Because your status was low? We have a lot in common then."

"Woof."

"Here, I have finished skinning the hare. Take the meat for yourself. I still have the caribou." Nauja tossed her the hare.

"Woof, woof."

She chomped the hare fiercely, turning it with her snout to get at a part she preferred. Three more times that sun, she placed a thin hare at his feet. Each time, he skinned the hare quickly and tossed her the carcass.

"You are making more work for me, Ktoh. Now I must process all these hides. Don't get me wrong, at the end of the light moons, I will be glad to have nice soft mittens, and liners for boots and maybe a warm hood. But until then, I'll have to process their hides and carry them with me."

A hand of suns later the caribou meat was gone. Nauja had started roasting the hares Ktoh brought him. However, she did not bring enough to feed them both. Nauja scoured the landscape for a caribou herd.

When the sun was high in the sky, Nauja saw a herd of high-horned musk ox. These beasts were far too large to kill on his own. His spear would not be able to penetrate the tough hide unless he got close. And without the tribe to keep the main herd away, this was not an option. He kept his eyes peeled for smaller game.

Assuming he could kill an animal with more meat than a skinny hare, Nauja thought about the stew he would make. It would consist of the sweet yellow wooly fern weed root he had found. He would add dried sage for an earthy flavor.

His life-pack was stuffed with sweet, yellow, wooly fern weed root. He wanted to add it to a pot of meat stew. He also needed a larger kill to provide him with a pot to cook his stew.

Meanwhile he sucked on the early fern weed blooms for their sweetness. Again, he had to thank his mother for raising him on roots and plants. He had learned to like them. The other boys teased him for snacking on the sweet roots. They only wanted to suck on dried caribou strips. Even what he ate seemed to be a reason for the other boys to taunt him.

When they passed the musk ox herd, Ktoh growled low in her throat. She left him for the first time that sun. She raced away from the herd and placed herself downwind of it. This way the herd could not smell her. Nauja watched in curiosity.

Despite her lack of motherly training, her instincts kicked in. She had also learned from the wolf pack. As the herd started to pass her by, she slunk low, creeping in, virtually unnoticed. A few of the cows looked her way, but a lone wolf would not have been a threat to the great beasts. Then Ktoh looked straight at Nauja. The blue eye glinted again, and Nauja felt the connection, the touching. He felt her question, "Are you ready?"

Nauja sprinted closer to her. *What am I supposed to be ready for?* he thought. Suddenly, she sprang out of her hiding place. She ran between a cow and her calf. She turned the frightened calf away from its mother and away from the herd. Then she forced it to run directly toward Nauja.

Nauja heard the bellowing of the calf's mother as well as Ktoh's growls, snarls, and that odd, clipped noise she made. Nauja had heard wolves bark, but the barks never came out as individual sounds. A wolf's bark was more like a short howl.

Although Ktoh's bark was an odd sound, Nauja could detect its meaning. It was almost as if Ktoh were telling him to go after the calf. She was telling him that she would distract the cow.

Without a second thought, Nauja ran in to thrust his spear with all his force hitting the calf directly in its neck. It fell clumsily to the ground. Sprinting to the fallen calf, he pulled out his cutting stone as he ran. He yanked his spear from the calf's neck and slit its throat.

The bellowing and growling stopped. Nauja wondered if Ktoh had been killed. He hadn't heard a death howl from her. But she might have been gored by the cow's sharp horn. Or she might have had her ribs shattered from a butt of a bull's head. As he slit the calf's belly open, he thanked both the musk ox calf for its life and Ktoh for making it possible to kill this great animal. Its hide, meat, bones, and small horns would be extremely useful. But he felt sad at the loss of his own animal.

When the bellowing of the calf had stopped, the herd went on its way. The loss of one young male was not a huge one. Nauja slowly skinned the large beast. *The skin will make a perfect tent covering for the next dark moons,* Nauja thought. *Ktoh might have been able to help me get another for a sledge platform. Or I could have made a small hut.*

He was thinking about the deep loneliness of spirit he would feel without the animal when he heard an insistent yip. He turned to see Ktoh looking straight at him, the blue eye sparkling again. She was demanding pay for her work.

"You will have to wait a bit, girl," he explained. "I want to get the hide removed before gutting it. That was very brave Ktoh. And very smart. Did the wolves teach you to cut a calf from the herd or did you once belong to a pack of your own kind?" he questioned as if he expected an answer. He hoped that by talking to her, he could delay her demand for payment. Skinning was hard work on such a large animal. He was also concerned about predators.

"Ktoh, that was such a great strategy. You are a good hunter, and I will reward you with half of the liver as soon as I gut this kill. It is your kill too. It was your idea. I couldn't have done it alone. I would not have even tried it. How did you know that I would understand to make the kill while you distracted its mother?

"I believe you must have a man's soul inside. Maybe that is what you are, a man-wolf. Maybe you have the soul of my sister who walks the wind." Ktoh just looked at him with her bizarre, differently colored eyes.

Finally, he had the huge skin separated from the ox. Now he could begin butchering the meat. He cut around the knee bones and split them from the thighs. Next, he cut around each shoulder bone and removed each of the short legs. As he tossed each leg onto the hide, Ktoh made no attempt to take the meat. She sat on her haunches, watching each move

h.c. Clarke

he made.

He slit down the backbone and removed the two long back straps. These are the two muscle groups that run the length of the spine.

Next, he opened up the gut sack and removed the heart and liver. He tossed Ktoh a piece of the liver, which she gulped down noisily. She chomped in delight and licked her paws afterwards. Lifting her head back to Nauja, she seemed to be asking politely for more. Nauja couldn't stop a laugh at her expense.

"You don't even chew your food long enough to taste it, yet there are parts you prefer. I surely would like to know where you came from and what kind of animal you are." She woofed quietly in response.

"Ahhh, are you wanting to be part of the conversation, or do you just want more meat? You know, Ktoh, I need to keep my eye out for more obsidian. Neither my cutting stone nor my spear points will last forever."

In answer, Ktoh woofed and then whined. She inched forward and nudged a musk ox leg but did not take it.

"Oh, so you want more, then? Your belly is not full? Here, have the rest of the liver. I need to take this boy's bladder to the creek over there to clean. It will hold more water than my small one. Do not gorge yourself when I am gone, or you will be sorry later."

Nauja cleansed and re-cleansed the bladder. His mother had told him more than once, "Clean all the food you eat thoroughly. I do not want to have my one surviving child die of sickness on his manhood trek." When he returned, Ktoh was in the same spot she'd been in when he left her. "Not even a young boy from the tribe would have been so well behaved."

Nauja tossed the meat onto the hide and rolled it all together. He cut a thin strip from the caribou hide and tied this second roll with the first one, that of the caribou skin. He slung the large bundle over his shoulder with an old man's "ummph" escaping from his lips.

"Come on then, Ktoh. If you are going to accompany me, we must be on our way. My search for a gift is still young. Although meeting face to face with a bear and her cubs, pounded by ice-rain, and threatened by a wolf-pack, followed by a she-wolf that is not really a wolf, and now killing a musk ox, I feel I have already had my share of adventure. I could do with a few suns of boredom. I think I will never have those again as long as you are with me."

Without looking back at her, Nauja started off, using the shaft end of his spear as a walking stick to help offset the heavy bundle on his back. Tonight, he would work on the musk ox hide and smoke the meat.

Before the sun was low in the western sky, her tall animal who wore the fur of others and had the long black mane of a horse, came to a small cave-like depression. He dropped the skin he had slung over his back but continued to walk around making his queer noises. *Apparently, he is searching for something. Might he be looking for water? Why can't he just smell it? I'll have to show him that water is near,* she thought. She scampered past him.

She returned to him and barked. Then ran ahead toward the creek and back to him. When he continued to ignore her, she stood in front of him and barked loudly this time. She nudged his body just a bit. "Hey. I have found the water you are looking for," she woofed.

How could this animal, who has so many other powers, not understand her pay-attention-to-me bark? Finally, he looked at her and made those queer noises he was always making. This time it ended in a higher note which she had learned was a signal he was paying attention to her.

He followed her to the creek she had found and made his "happy noise." It was as if he had found it all by himself. *Hah, he would have found it sooner if he had listened to me at the beginning.*

He returned to his bundle. He spread out the caribou skin and rolled the musk ox meat onto it. Then he dragged the heavy hide to the small creek. He made his weird noises from his flat snout the whole way. He was such a strange animal. He needed to make noise all the time.

She felt his need to make noise and to wear the fur of others sad. It made her feel that she had to take care of him. But she knew he was a superior animal. He could control Fire. He could even bring it into existence as well as kill it.

And by walking on only two feet, he could carry things in his top paws, and he could use sticks and rocks to modify his world. It would take a great effort on her part to train him in the ways of furred animals, but she felt he was worth training. They would make a good team, the beginnings of a good pack.

Chapter 7
A Delay in The Journey
Life is the flash of a firefly in the night.

He wanted to remain for the two suns allowed by Átenaq in order to process the hides and meat properly. When Ktoh showed him the small creek, he told her, "This will do nicely, Ktoh. We can put our backs against the rock with the fire in front. And that small grove of birch to the east will stop at least some of the wind. Yes, this will do well for now."

Nauja got to work. Ktoh watched. She growled when she thought he was doing something dangerous such as starting a fire. She whined if he did something she didn't understand. He started a fire under a branch of the largest scrub birch tree. He made sure it was not close enough to burn the tree or the branch. He placed all the meat on the caribou skin and took the musk ox hide to the creek, weighting it down with rocks.

He stripped off three thin branches from the tree. On two of them, he left a crook to make a fork, and from the third he stripped off all the side branches. Next, he walked back to the tundra and picked sage to flavor the meat. He made a hole in several pieces of musk ox meat and strung strips of caribou through the holes. He hung them from a branch. He added green wood to the fire for a nice flavorful smoke. He also periodically threw on sage.

Finally, he skewered a larger piece of meat to eat that night. The skewer stick rested on forked branches. It would help to feed the fire with its fat. Then he went back out to the tundra and gathered fist sized rocks of basalt.

Ktoh wanted to help and brought him a rock of the same size. Nauja looked at the rock, but it wasn't the strong basalt he needed. These rocks would crack too easily when heated. He showed Ktoh his own rock.

h.c. Clarke

"Like this one, Ktoh. Heavy gray with white flecks." He threw her rock away and put his rock in front of her. Ktoh ran to fetch another rock, understanding that it must be just like Nauja's. She fetched one and dropped it at his feet.

"Yes, Ktoh. That is the correct type of rock."

His thoughts immediately turned to Yuka. "Yuka will like you well enough, Ktoh. You are just as observant as she is. You learn quickly. And like Yuka, when you know the answer, you do not hesitate to assert your authority as you did when you showed me the spring or when you showed me how to get the musk ox. I would never have gone after a musk ox by myself. Their horns can easily gut and toss a hunter. They are fierce beyond words. Yes, Yuka will approve of you."

He placed the fist-sized stones right into the fire. He used a mattock he had made from a caribou antler to dig up the roots he wanted. This time Ktoh noted the ones he wanted.

She playfully ran back and forth until she spotted one. Digging with her claws, she pulled up each root and dropped it in front of Nauja. In a short period, he had enough, but Ktoh kept bringing him more. She barked and even growled if he did not want them.

Nauja cut a large square of the caribou skin. He used an awl he had also made from an antler to poke holes into the hide all along the outside. Next, he laced a small strip of the hide through one hole and out the next. When he pulled the ends, it gathered into a pot. He filled it with water and hung it from a tripod made of sticks.

When spread, the tripod held his pot so that it just touched the ground. The pot would have a flat bottom once the weight of the water was inside. He added the washed roots and chunks of meat and a bit more sage.

Nauja took each heated rock using flattened bone tongs he had made from two of the smaller musk ox bones scraped against a rock until flattened on one end and placed each rock into the pot. He took each out and put them back in the fire when cooled. While he waited for his pot to boil, he turned the meat over the fire or sliced the larger pieces into thin slices for drying. Good smells arose from the meat and roots in the pot.

Ktoh had splashed and played in the stream when Nauja was weighting down the musk ox hide and filling the stew vessel with water and then got bored. She whimpered for his attention. She growled. When he still ignored her, she ran off on her own.

At first, she got more rocks and roots, but when Nauja didn't want them, she ran off again. This time she didn't come back. Once he thought he heard her snarl, but he wasn't sure. When the sun started to sink in the west, he wondered if she had decided not to stay with him anymore.

I haven't felt this way since the beginning of my journey, he thought. *Ktoh, I didn't realize how much I rely on your company. I know it's your choice to stay or go, but that doesn't change how I feel. Maybe I should have paid more attention to you. I promise, I will try not to neglect your feelings again. Just come back to me.*

He was sad, but knew it was her choice to stay or go. When the meat was done, he only picked at it. He wasn't hungry anymore. Then he threw it back into the pot.

Suddenly he heard the bracken snap, and Ktoh proudly dropped a rabbit in front of him. She woofed happily, sitting down on her haunches waiting to be praised.

"You prefer rabbit over musk ox?" Nauja inquired. "Aren't you tired of rabbit? Or were you just bored, and it's fun to chase hares?"

Nauja and Ktoh stayed at the site for three suns. He knew it was against the rules, but Old Átenaq never thought that any of them would kill a musk ox. There was a lot of meat to process in addition to the huge hide. And besides, he had travelled more than a moon.

Once the hide was soaked and scraped of all its meat, Nauja poked holes at each corner of the soaked and scraped hide. Then he stretched it out to dry. He tied each corner to a frame he made from sticks. Next, he mashed a portion of the brain and made a thick paste by adding a little hot water.

He rubbed the paste into the hide. Before the paste had totally dried, he rubbed the paste in again. After the third time, Nauja started working it. He ran the bone back and forth across every inch. He pounded it with a bone or a rounded rock.

It was a long, boring process. Usually women did this work. But Nauja knew Yuka would make him help as his mother had made him and his father help. He had to rub and scrape, bend and rub, pound and rub. Pounding and rubbing loosened the fibers. The more it was worked, the softer it would be. Eventually it would become a soft cozy blanket or ready to sew into clothes.

The next new sun he found his burdens were too heavy. "This won't do, Ktoh. I cannot carry all this meat by myself." When he came to a grove of tall birch, he found a strong branch on the ground. He slit one end and gently separated it. He inserted his cutting stone and wrapped it with sinew in a crisscross pattern to hold the stone tightly. Now he had an axe. Then he searched the grove for a large branch with another off shoot. He needed to have a large branch with a fork[i].

He chopped down a tree about the same height as himself. Next, he chopped off all the smaller branches. He left one large branch. This created a fork. Next, he unrolled the musk ox hide and laid it over the space between the fork.

He lashed this tightly through the holes he had punched for the frame. He piled his meat and hare hides on top, tying them in tightly. Now he could drag his load without ruining the musk ox hide.

Patiently sitting on her haunches, Ktoh tilted her head one way and then the next.

---

[i] Technically, Nauja would not have used the word *fork* since forks had not been invented until 2100 BCE.

She watched everything Nauja did. She had seen her two-legged animal do many strange things, but this was the strangest.

You have powers I do not, so I will watch and wait to decide if I approve. If you are making something that will hurt you, I will stop you. Your life has become more important to me than my own, she thought.

You have made something to carry all the things your front paws cannot. I can drag one of those. I can help. It is my nature to help you. Figure out how I can help, or we will not continue.

When Nauja started off again, Ktoh would not stop barking. She placed her body in front of him, preventing him from walking. He stopped to look her. She went back to the grove of trees and started barking again.

"Do you want your own dragging sledge, Ktoh? Are you jealous of my new piece of equipment?"

Nauja returned to the grove and cut down a branch which had a fork in it. He then took what was left of his caribou hide and laid it across the space. *Now, how could he attach it to Ktoh?* he thought. She could not just hold the end and drag it the way he could. He stood staring at Ktoh and staring at the new smaller sledge.

Then he cut two strips of the caribou hide. He tied one to the dragging branch. With the other he made a loop to fit around Ktoh's belly. This he slipped over Ktoh's head and front legs. Then he attached the lead of the drag branch. But as she moved, the branch kept slipping to her side, putting the entire load out of balance.

Nauja just stood looking at the animal, the forked branch, and the lead to the belt-like loop around Ktoh. After fussing with the device, moving the lead to one side and then the other, he stood back again and stared at Ktoh.

"Hmmm, Ktoh. It seems we need a stick on both sides of your back to balance the load." He turned back to the birch trees. He found another branch of the same size.

He took apart the initial sled. He broke off the fork. He tied each of the larger branches to its own lead. He knotted these around Ktoh's belt loop. He spread the two branches apart, so each one fell to a different side Ktoh's body. Then he secured

h.c. Clarke

the skin from one branch to the other. As if she knew what Nauja wanted, Ktoh moved forward demonstrating how the whole thing would work when she walked.

Nauja's pleasure with the resulting product caused him to rebuild his own dragging sledge with two branches. He made a halter around his own shoulders behind his neck. *This will leave my arms free to carry other things or throw a spear,* he thought. He made the halter long enough that the branches could be tied at his waist. This would keep them from swinging against his body. He tied them again to his own waist belt. Ktoh barked several times and advanced forward glancing back at Nauja.

She seemed to be saying, "Ok, let's go now, lazy man. Don't just stand there staring."

"Ktoh, you never cease to surprise me. First you helped me kill a musk ox, then you found stones and roots. Now you want to drag whatever I drag. You are truly a worthwhile companion. Ok, on we go to find the next adventure," he answered.

A thought then occurred to him, *could this sledge halter be an invention worthy as a gift? Would it change the lives of my people? Yuka would think so because most of the dragging was done by women. There it is. There's my answer.*

The elders would not think a gift which lessens the work of only women to be valuable. That is why my mother's knowledge of plants was not deemed worthwhile. How callous men can be. I wonder if it will ever be different. Could we regard the work of women equal to that of men? If I gain a high status and marry Yuka, could the two of us effect a change this big?

Many suns later, as they were walked under the bright sun, Ktoh became overly distressed. She growled low in her throat, whined, and then she tipped her nose to the sky and released a long and troubled howl. Nauja was confused. She had never howled before.

"What is wrong, Ktoh? What do you smell? What do you hear? Are you calling to your kind? Do you hear them calling to you?" She howled into the wind again and Nauja could hear a faint return howl.

Chapter 8
In The Lion's Den

The bravery of a lion does not protect it from the spear of a hunter.

Nauja watched Ktoh for a moment, thinking. "If you want to rejoin your kind, Ktoh, I will not make you stay with me. It would not be fair to you. But I will miss you terribly." One lone tear made its way down his cheek. He turned away to hide his face as if she were a human.

Ktoh looked at Nauja and started barking. She slipped under her harness and ran ahead. She returned grabbing at his clothing and barking. She was visibly disturbed. "You aren't trying to leave me. There is a threat ahead and you want me to follow." Nauja followed Ktoh's lead and dropped the harness from around his own shoulders.

When she knew Nauja understood that he had to follow, she turned and ran ahead at top speed. Ktoh ran far ahead. Nauja ran as fast as he could to follow her. His spear was ready to throw.

"Ktoh," Nauja yelled. "Don't attack whatever it is you are chasing. Ktoh, stop. It isn't safe. We must avoid whatever beast it is."

Nauja had come to rely on Ktoh's skill in sensing danger. If she detected a threat, she made him go a different way. This time was different. This time she headed straight toward the danger. She wanted to join the fight whatever it was.

But Ktoh ignored her human friend. She ran ahead far faster than Nauja could hope to do. The snarling, growling and barking of two comparable animals grew louder. Nauja struggled to catch up. *Was she attacking a wolf or her own kind?*

As Nauja rounded a cliff, he saw the cave lion. It snarled and roared at the two comparable animals. It stood on a man but was too confused to finish the kill. Ktoh had joined another of her kind, a wolf-but-not-wolf. This one was snarling and growling at the beast. The two animals knew to work together.

h.c. Clarke

The animals took turns dashing into the lion's flanks. They were on opposite sides. Each nipped the lion and jumped away before the lion's paws could swipe. Ktoh was even more cruel in her attacks. It was as if she had a personal grudge against the beast.

The lion stood over the man. It wanted to kill him. These animals were in its way. Its snarls echoed throughout the site. It became angrier as the two animals took turns attacking the huge cat.

The man under the lion was yelling and screaming. He was holding up a spear across his body. But the spear would not protect him for long. One bite could snap the staff in two. Finally, Ktoh's partner succeeded in getting a huge chunk out of the cat's huge thigh.

The cat roared wildly. It turned to its attacker. It bit down on the scruff of the Ktoh-like animal's neck. It flung the wolf-like animal aside as if the large animal were no more than a flea.

The animal landed with a wail. Nauja's attention was on the man beneath the huge cat. He rushed in as close to the lion as he dared. He aimed carefully, and hurled his spear with all his power. The spear, with its sharp tip, flew towards its mark. The spear hit the cat. It pierced through the neck of the lion, and ended its life instantly.

The moment the lion collapsed; the man fainted. He had used up all his energy in screaming. He lay inert under the carcass of the giant cave lion. Nauja ran in but could not drag the cat's great body off the man.

"Ktoh, help me," he yelled to Ktoh. She was whining over the still body of the other animal. Nauja took hold of one of the cat's great paws and Ktoh grabbed the upper thigh of the same leg. In this way, they dragged the body off the unconscious man.

Nauja put his ear to the man's mouth. He listened for a breath. He could feel the heart beating beneath his fingers. At Nauja's prodding, the young man woke and tried to talk but was incoherent.

"Stay still, friend. I am here to help you," Nauja said. He wasn't sure if the young man understood. Gashes on each shoulder were deep but not bleeding much. *The beast must have been confused by the similar-to-wolf animal. This animal clearly travelled with the man as Ktoh did with me. I am sure Ktoh would do the same for me.*

Nauja ran back to Ktoh's sledge. He dumped the contents on the ground and grabbed the caribou skin. He also took his hide pot and tripod. Ktoh had run back to the big sledge with him and took Nauja's harness in her mouth, as if she knew he would want other items it held.

As Nauja ran back to the stranger. Ktoh grabbed the harness in her mouth. She dragged the entire sledge towards the scene of the attack. Nauja ignored her. He had to save the life of this stranger.

He dug a small hole in the ground. Then he laid the caribou hide into it. He sliced two wide strips from the caribou skin. Next, he poured water into the hole. He stuffed the strips into the water to soften them. Then he started a fire.

He found a fist-sized basalt rock and called to Ktoh, "More, Ktoh. Find more." She ran off to get more of the hard rocks. She dropped each one into the fire herself before taking off to find another. Nauja laid the softened hide strips over the wounds. Then he placed a heavy rock on top of each one.

"These will stop the bleeding while I get the things I'll need to treat the man," he said out loud to Ktoh.

He set up his tripod and pot. He dumped out the remaining stew, rinsed the pot quickly, and poured more water into it.

He set up his tripod and pot. He poured water into it and put in the hot rocks. He looked at the cuts left by the lion. *I've seen this kind of wound before. The wide deep scarring will keep him from lifting his arms ever again. How can I make the scars thinner?*

An idea came to him. He reached into his life-pack and took out his needle. He threaded a thin piece of sinew through it. He removed the strips of hide from the wounds and put them back into the water to re-soak. He pinched the edges of skin and sewed them together. He used the tiny stitches his mother had taught him to use.

Mother, I don't think you ever thought I would be sewing human skin with the needle you made me take. I was so ashamed when you made me learn to sew. The other boys laughed at me. They called me "girl" for many moons. They even laughed at father because he did not protect my manhood. Little did they know I might be saving a man's life with this 'woman skill'.

"I'm just glad you went back to sleep, my friend. I don't imagine my sewing through your skin would feel good," Nauja said to the young man.[i]

He crushed tiny willow stems and mixed them with sage. Then he added boiling water. "Mother says the sage will drive off the evil spirits that like to live in new wounds. Later, when the wound had healed, he would look for arnica. He would make a new poultice with this as well."

Explaining things to Ktoh helped him keep his attention on the process rather than on the wounds.

"According to Mother, Ktoh," said Nauja between her multiple trips to bring the things on his sledge to the campsite, "the sage will help drive off the evil spirits that like to live in new wounds. Later, when the wound has healed, we must look for arnica to add to the poultice. Mother says it's better than sage for healing but can't be used on open wounds."

Then he took a bit of his honey and gently rubbed it over and into each wound. He spread the willow and sage paste on top. Finally, he wrapped the soaked strips around each arm. When the strips of hide dried, they would tighten. Along with the stitches, the strips would close the wounds making them heal better.

Ktoh arrived. She had dragged Nauja's heavy sledge to the camp site. Nauja poured more water into his hide pot and added more willow stems. A willow bark tea would help with the pain and fever which was sure to follow. He would sweeten it with honey.

While the tea was brewing, Nauja turned to the Ktoh-like animal. There were two large bites holes on each side of its neck.

---

[i] Archeologists have discovered stone age skeletons who have had amputations and survived long after the amputation thus it can be assumed that people of that time sewed human flesh.

But it was not dead. Nauja assumed it had been with the man.

"So, Ktoh," he said. "Your kind enjoys being around men. I presume it will not bite me if I treat his wounds?" Ktoh woofed in response and came over to lick the wounds of the other animal.

"Are you telling me you know best how to help your kind? OK, let me pull him closer to the fire to keep him warm. When you are through, I will place a bit of the honey and the poultice I made on the bites. I do not think I can stitch a hole."

Before moving the new not-wolf animal, Nauja looked around to analyze the site. He knew he would have to stay until the man and his furred friend were both well. But he did not know how long this would be.

"Ktoh, I know Old Átenaq will forgive me for staying more than two suns. A man's life is more important than rigid rules over a boy's manhood journey. I have travelled an approximate number of the required suns. I have completed the goal of the rules. And I have already killed my own meat."

He surveyed the features of the stranger's campsite. It wasn't a bad site. Talking aloud helped him formulate an objective analysis. "It is fundamentally flawed. Those boulders on the west side of the site worry me. That is probably where the cave lion leaped down upon the man. He didn't see it coming. It was downwind, so his wolf-animal didn't smell it. That's important.

"There is a high cliff to the north. That's good. It's too high for a predator to attack from above. And that small stand of scrub birches will of a small wind break to the never-ending wind coming from the east. Less wind will lessen the dust as well as keep the fire from spreading. And there is a creek nearby; always an important part of any camp site.

"Did the lion have a mate? Will that mate come to avenge her companion? Ktoh, will you know when another lion is near? This man's wolf-animal couldn't. I should probably not rely on you to either."

h.c. Clarke

Nauja continued his one-way conversation with Ktoh. "The lion attacked from the west. Was this a fluke? Is the lion a smart beast? And if it is smart, then it's mate will surely plan on revenge. I am learning so much on this journey, Ktoh. It never occurred to me that a wolf could have a human soul and a lion could be intelligent.

"I'll have to think on these things more. I wish Yuka were here with us, Ktoh. She could help me think. I can express my doubts and indecision to her, and she would not judge me and call me less of a man. She would listen. I need to listen more carefully to you, Ktoh. You are Yuka in the body of a wolf. Maybe Yuka had a sister that did not live. I'll have to ask her when we get home."

Nauja cleared a spot away from the cliff. *We can rest safely between the cliff and the fire. Even if Ktoh doesn't smell the lion's mate, the fire should keep it away,* he thought. Then he gathered small pieces of wood. Ktoh had seen him do this virtually every evening. Always wanting to be helpful, Ktoh gathered the bigger sticks she knew he would soon want.

Next, Nauja took a stick from his current fire and set it on the kindling he had laid out. As the fire took hold, Nauja looked from one to the other. *Two fires? Could that be the solution? If I set two fires one at each end of our site, would that keep the lion's mate away?* This new idea excited him. He had found a solution through necessity as he had with Ktoh's sledge.

Quickly he cleared another space for a second fire to the east of the current. Now he had three fires going. *I will not need the first. It is too far away from the cliff and was built in a hurry. Already it is starting to char the low growth around it, wanting to spread itself out of control.* He soaked it with water from the nearby creek and spread the ashes to make sure it was out.

He unpacked his things from the big sledge and laid the large musk ox skin on the ground. He gently moved the stranger onto the skin. Then he dragged the skin between the fires and the cliff. Finally, he picked up the wounded animal and laid it down next to the strange man.

"I know that when I sleep, if I know you are beside me, it helps, Ktoh. I think it will be the same with this man and his companion."

The willow stem tea had simmered all this while, and Nauja was sure it was ready. He filled his small bladder with the hot tea and added a generous dose of honey. Raising the man's head, he dripped the tea into his mouth. The man stirred but did not waken. At least he was capable of drinking the brew. Nauja did the same for the animal. Despite the taste, the creature drank the tea, grateful for the moisture.

His mother was the only one in the tribe who believed in this tea. She always gave the tea to Nauja and his father when they weren't feeling well. She also put it on cuts or wounds. *I don't know if it helps. I know I always felt better after drinking it.*

Yuka watched every time his mother made it. She asked his mother many questions about the tea. But his mother could never answer any of them.

"It was a cure my mother taught me. Her mother had taught it to her. And her mother had taught it to her from the beginning of remembering," she would say.

Yuka always answered, "Then why don't any of the other women use it, Amaak?"

His mother always smiled and said, "Because the other women are not crazy like me."

These words were repeated many times each year. Maybe that is why Nauja liked Yuka. She talked with his mother. She never called her crazy as the other girls did. Yet he had heard his mother call herself crazy every time. But Yuka never repeated it.

Yuka rarely yelled. She was strong in a deadly quiet way. One time he had heard her yell at a group of girls saying, "She is not crazy. She has different ways because she came from a western tribe. Her mother was the gift Nauja's father brought back from his own trek because she knew how to use plants. But no one would believe her. I believe her," Yuka had said.

"And if you were smart, you would believe her too. Nauja gets better faster than anyone in the tribe. His wounds heal faster too. So there!"

One girl stood by Yuka's side. Yuka had turned and walked away as if she knew she had won the argument. Oomsa never said a word but silently followed.

Chapter 9
Sacha

**Sitting silently beside a friend who is hurting
may be the best gift to give.**

Nauja had done all he could. Now it was up to the stranger to fight off the spirits. The honey, the plaster, and the willow bark tea would help. While the young man slept, Nauja set up meat to roast over the fire. He put roots into the pot and added more water.

He added the roasted meat when the water was hot. Ktoh periodically licked the wounds of the man's animal. Once in a while the animal whimpered. This let them both know it was not yet walking the wind.

"Your new friend, Ktoh, is clearly your kind, but he looks different. He does not have your heavy fur and he is yellow. You are gray with those large patches of white. You look more like a wolf than he does."

Ktoh woofed and walked to the strange man, licking his face. Then she went back to the animal, sat on her haunches, and woofed again. Nauja couldn't help but chuckle despite the desperate situation. "You're right, Ktoh. I will tend to my kind and you can tend to yours.[i] I am not jealous. Well, maybe a little, but I understand."

He then sat at the man's head, dripping more tea between his lips. Nauja studied the new man. He was as unlike Nauja as the new not-wolf animal was to Ktoh. This man was shorter than Nauja was, and his legs were more muscular. He was lighter in skin color than Nauja.

The biggest difference was his face and hair. The man's head was rounder than his own without the high cheek bones of his own people. He had a broad nose but a low forehead. He had very round eyes. His own people's eyes, mainly when they grew old, were long and narrow as if they had been squinting into the sun for so long that they got stuck that way. And the man had brown wavy

---

[i] Scientific evidence suggests that dog saliva has some antibacterial properties.

h.c. Clarke

hair which was soft to the touch. It was unlike Nauja's straight coarse black hair.[i]

Where does this man come from? He does not look like a grown man. He looks more like me, my age. I wonder if the men of his tribe goon treks to prove manhood as those from my tribe do. If so, he could be from very far away. I must take good care of him or I will never find out the answers to my questions. And I have so **many** *questions.*

Nauja noticed that two teeth in the stranger's upper jaw were missing.[ii] Young animals should not be missing teeth. He might have had an accident. But an accident would result in missing teeth side by side. These are on different sides.

"What do you think, Ktoh. Does your friend have all his teeth? " Nauja called to Ktoh.

Nauja moved over to the animal Ktoh was tending and lifted the upper lip. "He has all his teeth as you do. And they look just as fierce as yours. Only my friend, here, has missing teeth.

I'm surprised his mother let him live. But she would not have known he would be missing these teeth until he was older. That is probably why she did not make him walk the wind when he was born."

Nauja had a lot of time to think while taking care of the stranger. He thought about the past two moons of experiences. He thought about what he had learned.

First, I had to learn how to take care of myself. I had feed myself, make every decision all by myself. Those were the words of Old Átenaq, "If you cannot feed yourself, you cannot feed the tribe and we do not want you back." Those were his words.

Then I was ready to take care of another. I met Ktoh. I saved her from starving. And we learned from each other. I

---

[i] DNA evidence shows that remnants of the Jamōn people still exist in northern Japan.

[ii] Ritual tooth ablation was practiced by the Jamōn and Yayoi cultures of Japan, from 13,000 to 2,300 years BPE.

had to learn the ways of a wolf, what she wanted, what she needed, and all the different meanings of the different barks she has in her own language.

Now I can tell when she is warning me of danger, when she is happy or when she smells food ahead. Although we have become a team, she knows that I am in charge. I am her chief. She trusts me to make the right decisions.

Nauja sighed. Ktoh came to his side, leaving her own charge. "You trust me so totally, Ktoh. I must listen to you before making a decision that involves you. I would not be a good leader if I did not think about your well-being as well as my own. Maybe even above my own," Nauja said to the animal as she laid by his side. She made sure her body touched his for the full length of her back. Nauja's hand began to stroke her fur, giving both of them quiet pleasure.

"Now I have another *man* to save. This other man depends on me to make the correct decisions for both of us. He is a stranger. I could leave him and go on my way. I still have a gift to find for my tribe. This man is delaying me. But I feel I must stay. Something is making me put his needs above my own."

The young man's fever broke two suns later. He slowly opened his eyes. He stared closely as Nauja took off the hide bandages. He soaked them in warm willow tea. He applied a fresh poultice and then put the bandages on again. *There has been no pus,* he thought. *That means there are no evil spirits.*

Nauja pointed to himself and said, "Nauja." Then he pointed at the young man.

"Sacha," the young man responded and pointed to himself. "Gohan, Yoi." Pointing to the stew and clay bowl, he smiled his gap-toothed grin and rubbed his hand on his stomach. "Yoi," he repeated.

"You are hungry and are looking forward to your meal. That is good. 'When the appetite returns, the patient is on the mend.' At least that's what my mother says."

Nauja took a small vessel he had made from clay while waiting for Sacha to wake. It was not a very good bowl; he did not have the best clay to use. But it hadn't cracked when he fired it, and it did hold enough stew for a small meal. It was certainly better than the hide bowl he had made for Ktoh. As Nauja was scooping up the stew, the young man said something in a language Nauja did not know. Some words seemed to raise and lower in pitch.[i] He pointed to his own things and subsequently brought his fingers to his mouth to illustrate eating.

Nauja got the pack for Sacha. The young man opened the hide flap and took out a pouch. He handed it to Nauja. Each time he moved his arm, Nauja could see pain on the young man's face. Nauja looked inside and saw long brownish-black seeds that looked almost like skinny insects or charred larva.

Sacha motioned him to put a handful in the stew pot. Nauja started to scoop out stew again. Again, Sacha stopped him. Sacha put one elbow on his other arm and pointed up to the sun. Then moved that hand slowly until it reached the arm it was resting on.

"I know what you're saying; the sun moving towards the horizon. Oh, you want me to wait a bit after putting this in the pot. I presume you will tell me when?"

Sacha seemed to understand. He bent his head down and then up. He stared at Nauja to see if Nauja understood. "Well, my new friend, it appears nodding one's head, like pointing, is the same in both our languages.

"Gohan," Sacha said pointing to the pouch of seeds. He then said, "Yoi," pointing to the stew and clay bowl. Then he smiled his gap-tooth grin and rubbed his hand on his stomach. "Yoi," he repeated.

"There are many gestures we can use to talk with, my new friend. And I recognize some of your words. Perhaps our people came from the same place long ago?"[ii]

Sacha tried to sit up. Nauja gently put his hand on the young

---

[i] Research suggests that tonal languages developed only 6000 years ago, therefore only some of Sacha's words would be tonal.

[ii] Jōmon share closer a relationship to the Ancient Northeast Asian/Eastern Siberian and Native American cluster than the Southern East Asian.

man's chest. He said, "No, my friend. You must rest. The fever has broken, but your wounds have not healed." Then he remembered the gesture Sacha had used to imply wait. Nauja pointed to the sun with arm bent at the elbow. He slowly moved it downward. Sacha understood. He laid back down on the musk ox skin. He rubbed the fur of the hide and pointed at Nauja indicating his surprise that Nauja was able to kill the musk ox by himself.

Nauja pointed to Ktoh. He told Sacha the two of them killed the great beast together. Then he acted out the kill as best he could, and Sacha seemed to understand.

Nauja wanted to know more about the animal that was with Sacha. This was the most important thing. He pointed to Ktoh's new friend. Nauja inquired, "Sacha, what is your animal?"

"Dog," Sacha replied understanding immediately.

"Is that his name or the kind of animal he is?" Nauja tried to ask. Sacha did not understand. Nauja pointed at himself and said, "Nauja." Then he pointed to Ktoh and said, "Ktoh." Next, he pointed to Sacha and said, "Sacha." Finally, he pointed to Sacha's animal and raised his arms halfway up pointing the palms outward, "Who?"

"Dōshi," Sacha replied. To make it clear, Sacha pointed at Ktoh and Dōshi using both hands and repeated, "Dogs." He pointed at each one and repeated their names, "Ktoh, Dōshi."

Ktoh understood. She walked to Dōshi and licked his face. Sacha laughed. Then Sacha pointed at Ktoh and again at his own animal, laughed again, and said, "Mieto."

When Nauja indicated that he did not understand, Sacha pointed back and forth several times to Nauja and then to himself and said, "Tomadachi." Then pointed back and forth from Ktoh to Dōshi saying, "Mieto."

Nauja was confused. Sacha seemed to have complicated his question. He still did not understand. The dogs are friends and he and Sacha are friends. Why is there an alternative word when the friends were animals? *Well, who am I to judge other languages? Sacha probably feels the same way about my language.* Sacha laughed again and repeated the gesture for wait, pointing at the sun moving his hand at the elbow.

Nauja then asked his next burning question. Pointing to his own teeth and then to Sacha's, he asked, "Why do you not have a full set of teeth?"

Sacha smiled widely, showing his missing teeth. He said something that Nauja did not understand at all. Sacha moved his hands to his teeth. He pretended to yank them out. Then he offered the pretend teeth to Nauja.

"You pulled them out on purpose as a gift? What motive could you have to do such a thing?" Nauja asked in horror.

Sacha puffed out his chest, stiffened his back, and pulled in his stomach. He said "O toko." Sacha o toko. This time Nauja understood.

"You do this when you become a man?"

Nauja pointed to himself and used the sign for wait. Then moved his fingers to indicate walking. Then he lifted his hand to his eyes to show searching. Finally, he used Sacha's gestures for giving.

They spent the hands after high-sun talking to each other. They traded words and used gestures until Nauja noticed that Sacha was getting tired. Nauja put his hands together at one ear pantomiming sleeping and gently pressed his hand on Sacha's chest. Sacha agreed and lay back down on the fur of the musk ox skin. In no time, he fell asleep, his hand on Dōshi's back
.

Chapter 10
A Decision to Make

Whether we walk among our people alone, happiness in life's walking depends on how we feel about others.

A hand of suns later, Sacha was fully healed. While Nauja pulled out the stitches, he gritted his teeth but remained silent. There was not much else to do around the campsite except talk. They learned a lot of each other's languages. They formed a close friendship.

They had learned that each was on a manhood trek. This was part of becoming an adult. They drew maps on a cleared section of the ground to show where each had come from.

"My people are called the Jōmon. It is an island far to the south.[i] I used a boat to travel across the sea to the west and I have walked for more than a moon." Sacha drew a picture of a boat when Nauja did not understand.

"Boats? My people fish, but we do not use boats. Water is dangerous. It kills, and to go so far when you can't just walk to shore would be unheard of!" Nauja replied, his eyes getting rounder.

"Ha ha," Sacha laughed. "You should see your eyes. They are almost as round as mine. Don't your people learn to swim? If you fall into the water, you can swim to the boat. The water is not cold during the warm season where I come from."

"No, my people do not learn to swim. My mother taught me to swim, but the other women laughed at her. They told her that she would lose the only child she managed to keep alive for more than a few moons. They called her Crazy Woman," Nauja admitted. He looked to see if Sacha thought she had been crazy too.

Am I risking my new friendship telling Sacha about my mother? I don't know why, but I feel he will not laugh.

"Why in the world would they call her crazy? She was

---

[i] During the last ice age, Japan was part of the mainland and not an island.

h.c. Clarke

doing the right thing to keep her child safe. I think your mother should be called Unusually-Smart-Woman. Look how she taught you to care for me. You saved my life, Nauja of Beringia. You are my brother, and I will always owe you a great debt."

Uneasy with this praise, Nauja changed the subject. "Why do you say unusually smart? Don't you think women are as smart as men?"

"What a silly question, Nauja. Of course they are not as smart as men. They are meant only for work men do not want. And to have more men, of course.

Now he sounds like the men of my tribe, thought Nauja. I thought he would be different. I wonder what he would do if I argued with him. Is it worth losing our friendship? But then is a friendship worth having without honesty?

Sacha realized he might have hurt his new friend, "I apologize, Nauja. I should not have called your question silly. You asked a question. I should answer it."

Sacha's apology gave Nauja courage to speak up. "Yes, Sacha. I do believe women are just as smart as men. If we would listen to them, men would realize it. I think it is our desire to have someone to boss around that makes us say they are not as smart as we are. But maybe that's a discussion for another time.

"Tell me about how you got your dog. I want to know everything about them."

"When I arrived over the sea, I stayed with a tribe that had many dogs," Sacha explained. "The people there said they had owned dogs since time began. The dogs were helpers in many ways. The people said a dog is a man's best friend because they give their love unconditionally.

"They said dogs would help hunt. Dogs kept children safe when they were left alone. And they not only warned of danger but defend you 'til death. Finally, they said that in starving times, dogs could be eaten if necessary. I witnessed many of these incidents during the short time I stayed with them.

"One time, a dog found a child who had been lost. And one time a dog rescued a man when he was drowning. The dog swam out to the man who held onto the dog's fur and the dog swam back to shore with him."[i]

Nauja looked at Ktoh with more and more respect. *And to think Ktoh chose me as her person. But I guess we chose each other. I would never have saved the life of a wolf if it had come to my camp starving. I would have thanked it for its skin as I did with the caribou and the musk ox, but I wouldn't have saved its life. Ever since our souls touched, we hear each other's hearts.*

Sacha and Nauja decided to continue together. Sacha wanted to go north. He wanted to see the great ice mountains. He said no one had been as far north as he had already come. Then he said, "But you saved my life, so if you want to continue south, I will go with you."

"I don't mind returning north as long as we go west of the great ice mountains. There is a break between them. But I'm afraid we might not make it through the ice mountains before the endless night begins. If we go north, we may be spending the dark-moons in the ice cliffs, Sacha. In that case, we will need to have many more thick skins like my musk ox skin. And we will need mammoth bones to hold them up. Where I come from there is not much snow even in dark moons, but it gets terribly cold, and meat is scarce. I cannot imagine what it will be like in the mountains."

"What are these dark moons you speak of?" asked Sacha.

"What do you mean what are the dark-moons? They are the moons when there is no light."

"Many moons without *any* sunlight?" asked Sacha. "I've never heard of a place where the sun doesn't shine." His eyes expanded, getting rounder than usual.

"It's the opposite of now when there is very little dark.

---

[i] Studies have pointed to both Europe and China as the location of the first domestication of dogs, but neither has been proven. A third location entered the dispute when a 47,000- year-old canid from what was western Beringia was found which is distinct from wolves but only a few mutations away from modern dogs.

h.c. Clarke

Don't you have light moons and dark moons?" asked Nauja.

"No, we always have many hands of light. Yes, the suns are shorter in what we call winter, and longer in what we call summer, but we *always* get both light and dark."

"How strange," Nauja commented. What a wonderful place that must be, he thought to himself.

"And why do you need mammoth bones to hold up the house? Why can't we just use wood poles? My people do. Then we thatch the sides," Sacha said, putting his fingertips together with the palms spread out. The smoke goes out of a hole in the top because of the shape of the house. My people have been using houses like this since the time before remembering. They are easy to pack when we move to new hunting grounds," Sacha argued.

"But where do you suggest we find trees big enough for these poles you speak of? And where will we find grass longer than your hand?" Nauja asked quietly. He smiled at his own sarcasm and his new-found ability to tease a friend.

"Oh," said Sacha, looking around at the barren tundra landscape. "You have a point. How do you build houses in your tribe?" he inquired.

"First you dig down until you reach the permafrost. That's about the depth of your knees. Then you use mammoth and mastodon ribs to create the structure. Caribou antlers or even the ribs of the wooly rhinoceros can be used. These are covered with skins. They have to be sewn tightly. They can't let even a puff of cold air enter the house," replied Nauja.

"What is this ground you call permafrost?" asked Sacha.

"It's the depth at which everything is frozen all of the time."

"Hmmm. It sounds like a lot of work. Maybe we will find a friendly tribe to winter with. One that already has a house ready for us to occupy," laughed Sacha. "Many of my tribe have wintered with other tribes on their journeys," Sacha suggested.

"We can walk through the night with just a few hands for rest and sleep. There are not many dark hands I've noticed. This must be what you call light moons. Do you think we can clear the mountains before winter sets in."?

"You mean dark-moons? What you refer to as winter? But our burdens are many and will increase as we make big kills for skins." Nauja argued. He was not against returning north, but the ice mountains were intimidating, and he wanted to visit a land where the sun shines all year long.

"Then we will harness up both dogs to a large sledge like yours. They are both strong and muscular. They could most likely haul as much as we can, maybe more," Sacha reasoned analytically.

Nauja reminded himself that he had to think of the needs of others equally to his own. "Yes, Sacha, I think that could work."

They changed Ktoh's sledge leads to allow Dōshi to be harnessed next to her. The drag poles were attached on each open side of a dog. They made the frame larger because two dogs would now be pulling it. Nauja and Sacha would take turns pulling Nauja's smaller sledge. If they needed more than one drag sledge, they would make another.

The two dogs were excited to start the journey. They liked being harnessed together. They easily pulled the large sledge. They could go faster than either Nauja or Sacha. When there was something in their path, one dog pulled the other to avoid it. They knew that the legs of the new sledge would get caught or dump the load.

Ktoh would yip and snap at the Dōshi when she felt him getting lazy. This always made Nauja and Sacha laugh wildly.

"She reminds me of Yuka, the girl I will choose to be my mate," Nauja said between his fits of laughter. "I think the world of Yuka. But she is perfectly capable of keeping others in line."

They walked almost until dark. If there was enough light to see the ground, they continued their trek north. Many suns later, they entered an opening. It was a huge corridor between the two huge ice masses.

Each evening they camped and talked. It was easier for Sacha to learn Nauja's language than it was for Nauja to learn Sacha's tonal one. Each time Nauja tried to say something, Sacha teased him. What he said was not what he wanted to say. But Nauja continued to try.

When Sacha teased him, Nauja replied the same way. "I may sound foolish speaking your language, but I will wait until age takes my teeth, rather than giving them up on purpose."

Laughing, Sacha answered, "You need a gift for your tribe. Just give them your teeth. Then you won't have to worry so much about your gift and just enjoy your journey, like me."

Chapter 11
The Corridor of Ice

In any great task, it is not enough to depend simply upon yourself.

They talked around their campfires. They talked about their tribes. They shared customs and traditions. They took turns telling the stories and songs of their people. They had storytelling contests which ended in laughter. They had to force themselves to remain quiet to fall asleep.

Nauja had never felt so close to another young man. He wasn't this close with Raven. All he had felt in his life was bullying. He found the friendship he had wanted in Sacha.

Sometimes they talked of serious things. They shared their past failures. They also talked about their goals. For the first time, Nauja told another person his feelings about Yuka.

Sacha had never considered that a mate might be a partner. His people regarded women solely for their ability to produce more men. As before when this topic arose, Sacha sat quietly listening to Nauja.

"With Yuka, I can show when I am sad, or when I care deeply about a topic. You cannot do that with another man. He will laugh and call you weak.

"With Yuka, I can be myself. I do not have to pretend to be who someone else expects me to be. I can tell her I am scared to go out with the other hunters. Mammoths are dangerous. There is a risk that I may die."

Sacha was surprised. "What did she say? I have felt afraid whale hunting. But I would never tell anyone."

"She told me fear is a good thing. It keeps men alive; not because they avoid danger when they are afraid, but because they are wiser when they are afraid.

"'Fear gives us focus,' she said. 'When we are afraid, we

h.c. Clarke

see other ways of doing things. And when we see new ways, we save not only ourselves but others as well.'

"She said that is why our tribe makes us look for new things to bring back from our treks. My mother was my father's gift to the tribe when he returned from his trek. She pointed out that my father and I get sick less. Our wounds heal faster. Yuka's explanation was that my mother knows the secrets of plants. Others in the tribe have only scorn for plants. She said if the only thing that is different between other men and you is eating plants, then eating plants is obviously a good thing. The Woman-Who-Likes-Plants was an excellent gift.

"She also said fear gives us energy. Once I was running a race and I was winning. But my friend, Raven, was right behind me. Just before the end of the race, Raven surged forward ahead of me.

Yuka told me that it was because Raven had been afraid, I would win. He is Grandson-of-chief and would be shamed if he had lost. His fear gave him the energy to pass me by."

"That might be true," replied Sacha. One time a man fell out of a boat while we were killing a whale. He couldn't reach his boat because the whale was there. After struggling and screaming until he was tired, he suddenly got quiet and headed for another boat. We were all amazed that he swam to the other boat so fast."

"But the most surprising thing Yuka told me," said Nauja, "was that fear is the only thing that makes men ask for help. She said, 'Women accept each other's help often. Men want to appear so strong. They don't like to accept help. But they will accept help when they are afraid.

"I was amazed that a girl so young knew so much. I started watching her. I noticed that when she gave her opinion, they were always supported by facts. But others would not listen just because she is a girl. That is not right.

She had ideas and she had proof to back them up.

"We should listen to women. They think about things. They share their thoughts more than men. This way they get feedback from others. And then others add a detail to that idea. Men just want to boast of their prowess, their success in hunts."

Sacha was amazed at this new thought. He rubbed his finger behind his ear. Then brought it to his chin. "That is the gift you should contribute to your tribe, Nauja. You have convinced me that women might be more than producers of additional men.

"You must convince your tribe. If you succeed in converting them, you will have doubled not only the membership of your tribe but its wisdom as well.

"When I go home, *if* I go home, I will look at women in a new light. I will search out a smart woman like yours. I will look for a woman who thinks about more than caring for children and cooking rice. You have just given *me* a great gift. You should give the same gift to your tribe."

"I have tried, Sacha. My father has tried. No one will listen. They do not want to think that women could be equal to men. Even the weakest or lowest of men feels he is better than women. He would not want to give up that power easily.

"But what were you implying when you said, '*If* I go home?' Are you considering not going back to your people?"

"Yes. How could I go back and pretend that I have not changed? It is not easy to convert people to new ideologies. How could I go back and feel that I am better than women? I will at least go with you to your tribe. I want to see a land where the sun sleeps during winter."

But their conversation ended in laughter when Sacha added, "I think I am in love with your Yuka, Nauja. Maybe I will have to challenge you for her when we arrive at the lands of the People of Beringia." He jumped up and positioned his feet apart and arms bent with his fists clenched, ready to fight Nauja.

h.c. Clarke

The next sun, when it was high in the sky, both Dōshi and Ktoh started to growl. Dōshi stopped in his tracks with ears perked up. Ktoh pulled toward her side of the sledge. She pulled to the side with all her strength. Dōshi looked at her and followed her lead.

They both broke into a frantic run, moving the sledge toward the north wall of ice. Ktoh barked at Dōshi and loosed herself from her harness. Dōshi understood what Ktoh wanted. He continued to pull the sledge toward the ice sheet while she returned to the young men who were standing stock-still watching the odd behavior of the two dogs.

Ktoh got behind them and started nipping at their legs. She even pushed them toward Dōshi. Her nips became more desperate, and her barks became growls. Nauja and Sacha looked at each other in amazement. But each had learned to trust their dogs. They sprinted toward Dōshi and the sledge.

Then they heard it. Felt it. A great earth-shaking rumbling. It was as if the thunder were in the ground. They barely reached the ice wall when the rumbling became so loud, they could not hear each other even when shouting.

The great herd of woolly mammoth, tusks spearing the air ahead of them, came racing down the corridor. They were running for their lives. The trumpeting of the cows trying to locate their calves and the bawling calves trying to locate their mothers filled the air. The bulls were roaring to all behind them.

The older members of the herd were simply trying to catch up. They waved their huge tusks back and forth in fear. The result was one massive roar. It echoed off the walls of the ice sheet.

Dust and small rocks from beneath the feet of the great beasts pelted the boys like an attack from a hostile tribe. The young men faced the wall to protect their faces. Both yelled to their dogs in hope of hearing a response. They wanted to know that the animals still lived.

Ktoh was worried about Nauja. Nauja was worried about her. She pressed herself up against the backs of Nauja's legs. His upright body assured her that he was still alive, and she was determined that he stay that way. She leaned her weight against him, forcing him to press his face and belly into the wall of ice.

Finally, the roaring, trumpeting and general chaos slowed. But the older mammoth at the back were afraid. They moved back and forth. They were desperate to keep up with the heard. They were crazed with fear. Only in the main body would they feel safe.

Ktoh would not let Nauja move. Dōshi was keeping Sacha pinned to the ice wall too. Without warning, one huge bull approached. Despite the furious growls of both Ktoh and Dōshi, the huge body came within a man-length of the young men hugging the ice wall.

Suddenly Nauja heard a loud crack. A glance to his side revealed a massive tusk striking the wall to his right. The creature looked directly at Nauja. For a split second he saw the terrified look of the old beast. It no longer seemed a monster, just a scared old man. Then it turned away to follow its herd. For the first time, Nauja felt pity for these great beasts.

It must be hard to grow old as an animal. They have no family to look after them. Old animals die from our spears or a pack of wolves. An old animal does not die peacefully among its family, he thought. The best that an animal could hope for is to simply give up when it becomes too old to go on.

The charge finally ended. Nauja and Sacha walked between the dead animals. Nauja saw many saiga antelopes among the mammoth. These animals were built for speed with long thin legs and small size. They were not built to take the beating of the great beasts. They were built for speed with long thin legs. Their skins and meat were useless. Even their horns were crushed into bits and pieces by huge feet.

The young men did find several mammoth bodies worth collecting. The meat, horns, and hides were still whole. Now their worry about a shelter for the dark moons diminished. They started to butcher the animals. But they saw the reason for the stampede.

Hunters from a tribe beyond the ice mountains came running down the corridor. They were holding spears high. They were not going to let their kills be stolen by strangers.

Sacha was more articulate than Nauja. He dropped his spear and extended a hand to the hunters. He hoped he could show friendship by his broad smile. He spoke first in his own language and then in Nauja's. But the hunters did not understand either. They continued to shake their spears.

"Do you know these hunters, Nauja? If you do, step forward now or we will join the beasts lying around us," cried Sacha.

Nauja had had experience in avoiding conflict. He dropped his spear. He swept his arm over all the dead animals and pointed to the hunters. He hoped they would understand that the boys knew that it was not their own kill.

The hunters came forward, spears down and smiles on their faces. They pointed to the crushed bodies and then pointed to the boys. They laughed at their own joke of giving away useless kills.

Nauja and Sacha laughed too. It was a funny joke. So all was good between the hunters and the two young men. Nauja got out his cutting stone and pantomimed collaborating to butcher the animals. Then he pointed to the dogs and the sledges. He hoped the hunters would understand that they were willing to help. And that they could bring the meat to their community.

One hunter saw the dogs and raised his spear. He intended to kill what he thought was a wolf. Sacha saw the man raise his spear and threw himself towards the man. The man fell, and his spear flew wildly missing the two dogs.

When he looked up there were many spear points almost touching his chest. He was trying to explain when Nauja saw Dōshi sprinting toward his master. The dog was not going to permit an attack on his human.

"Sacha," yelled Nauja. "Stop Dōshi!"

Chapter 12
The Pillars

The ground on which we stand is sacred ground.
It is the dust and blood of our ancestors.

"Sacha," yelled Nauja. "Stop Dōshi!"

With many spears barely above his skin, Sacha yelled, "Dōshi SIT!" The animal did as he was told. The strangers were obviously amazed. But many spears were raised again, this time pointing at the dog.

Nauja quickly stepped in and tried to explain that the dogs were not wolves. Nauja showed the hunters Ktoh's harness. He then called his own dog.

"Ktoh! COME."

She came right away and sat in front of Nauja. She had her back to the many spears pointing directly at her. The hunters saw that the wolf-like animals were not dangerous. Spears lowered for a second time. Their leader gave a loud whistle at the sound of which many women and older children appeared almost out of nowhere from the ice wall where they had been standing during the stampede.

Help in the huge task of skinning and butchering the great beasts was always accepted. Their leader gave a loud whistle. At the sound, many women and older children appeared almost out of nowhere. They had been standing against the ice wall during the stampede.

Many hands of the sun later, Nauja and Sacha followed the hunters to their village. Both sledges were piled high with meat and skins. It took many trips to bring in all the meat, bones, and tusks. By the time they were finished, Nauja had picked up the small differences between their language and his own.

As they came near, they couldn't take their eyes off the view ahead. There were great columns of rock along the river as far as

h.c. Clarke

the eye could see.

Nauja remarked upon these shapes. "You did not accurately your home. What do you call those rocks? Do you know anything about them? How did they form? Have you explored them?"[i]

"How can we answer one question if you keep asking more without stopping to take a breath?" one hunter exclaimed, laughing.

"I can't help it," replied Nauja. "They are just so ... so... so I don't know. I don't have the words to describe them."

The hunter had to get control of his laughter. He patted Nauja on the back. "We are called the Pillars of The Ancestors Tribe. Yes, they are breath taking, aren't they? Our people have lived here since the beginning of time. Those pillars have grown. And more have appeared. They are the souls of our ancestors. So, you can see how long we have lived here," said another hunter.

"Each pillar is a family. They go back to the time before remembering. When our lives are over, we will join our pillar. Each of us knows where we will go to when our life ends. We will watch over our children and their children. We can watch everyone," the first hunter said.

"That's why we are such brave people. We do not fear death. No matter what happens to us in our lives, we will join our ancestors to watch over those that still live," the second hunter chimed in.

"As long as we live beneath them," added another of the hunters.

"That is true," the first replied. "If a person moves away, he or she cannot integrate with the pillar of their family. No one leaves the tribe. They want to be able to watch those that follow. It is a sad thing to have a member leave, sad for us, but more sad for *them*.""

---

[i] Lena Pillars is a natural rock formation along the banks of the Lena River in far eastern Siberia. The pillars are 490-980 ft. high.

Nauja and Sacha were amazed at the size of tribe. The pillars had affected the people in a profound way. It was clear that no one wanted to leave. Each member looked forward to the time when they would watch over their grandchildren.

The community was like Nauja's. The huts were dug into the ground. One building was larger than the others. *That must be the chief's lodge,* thought Nauja.

A group of elders approached the hunters.

"I see you have brought back more than mammoth meat, Evgi" an elder said.

"Yes, Honorable Elder. We met these strangers in the ice corridor. They are on manhood journeys. They are travelling together yet are obviously not from the same tribe," the man named Evgi said.

"I can see that! Why are they with you?"

"They helped with the butchering, and their animals helped haul everything home," Evgi added.

The Elder looked at Nauja and Sacha. He approached Nauja, "You look more like us than that one," he said, pointing rudely at Sacha. "Where are you from?"

"I am from Beringia. It is on the other side of the mountains where the world ends," responded Nauja. He looked the old man straight in the eye. He was angry when the man rudely pointed to Sacha.

"Well, we want to repay you for your help. You and your, um, follower are welcome to spend the dark-moons with us."

The boys accepted. It solved the problem of what to do during the endless night. Each had been worried about what to do, but neither had shared their worry with the other.

Nauja and Sacha were led to a structure as big as the chief's lodge. It was for young men without mates.[i]

"Women live with their parents until they are joined,

---

[i] Archeologists at Mal'ta excavated a structure that measured 46 feet long by 19.5 feet wide.

h.c. Clarke

but men should be independent," Evgi said. "If a man does not want to choose a mate, he moves into this lodge. He will live here until he has the maturity for a family of his own."

Nauja was a little tense. He had expected to be given a guest hut. When he had seen signs of people, he had changed directions. But Sacha was more outgoing. He was glad to be with young men from other cultures.

Luckily, the eligible bachelors' hut was located at the edge of the community. Nauja and Sacha built a pen for their dogs. They felt it was for the protection of dogs more than the people. It took several suns to convince people that the dogs were not dangerous.

When the people realized the dogs were safe, they couldn't stay away. The boys had to have strict rules that no one was allowed to come near them without either he or Sacha with them. It was more for the protection of the dogs from the people than it was for the people from the dogs. Everyone was curious about these people-loving beasts, but more than a few were afraid and felt they should be killed.

Nauja spent the short suns studying this tribe. He still needed to find a gift. Nauja concluded that this community had nothing of value. He was getting worried about finding a proper gift.

Because he wandered about alone, the elders viewed Nauja as the leader, despite his youth. Why else would he spend so much time alone? This made them very curious about the boy. They paid him respect that he didn't feel he deserved. They questioned him about his journey. They wanted to know what commodities other boys had found on previous treks. What was Nauja looking for? They would repeat questions either for clarification or if a new elder joined the group.

"Look how this Sacha of the south follows you, Nauja of Beringia," they said. "Many of our own young men have come to us with requests to follow you. They want a trek of their own. They do not want to stray from the Ancestors forever, but they want to travel."

Some of the other young men came to Nauja asking his opinion on this or that thing.

Nauja felt as if his brain had been picked clean by knowledge vultures. They didn't care about Sacha's tribe. It was too far away to matter. They did not feel that Sacha had an influence on others. He was friendly and sociable, but these traits did not constitute a leader of men.

Sacha chatted with other young people. He wanted to test Nauja's theory that women were as smart as men. He paid attention to the girls who answered his questions without turning their eyes to the ground. He also watched those who asked him questions in return. He looked for girls who invented new ways to do things.

Most early twilights, both Nauja and Sacha learned to make the beautiful carvings so prized by the people of The Pillars. They learned the stories and songs and even had story-telling contests with the other unmated men. Sacha never took offense at the teasing he got about his missing teeth but joined in with the laughter and always returned light insult for insult.

One night, Nauja complained to Sacha, "The elders asked me the same questions over and over again. I feel that they are not just elders, but too elder."

"I do not envy you," said Sacha, laughing at Nauja's pun. "You are setting yourself apart, Nauja. They look to you as a leader of men. I have never felt the need to be a leader. I am happy to let others make the decisions.

"But you have gained as much knowledge from them as they have from you. Finding out what people do not know is just as important as what they do."

Chapter 13
The Dogs
There are many great voices, but not all are human.

Nauja and Sacha demonstrated how Ktoh and Dōshi split a caribou from the herd. Dōshi, being larger and more threatening, turned to the herd, nipping at this or that animal's legs, while Ktoh herded the stray away. They did this many times. The whole tribe was busy skinning and butchering the large animals. Even the children were hauling the butchered parts back to the village. There the meat was sliced for smoking and drying. With all the meat brought in that season, there would be no starving times.

The elders decided to hold a feast. Several caribou and elk calves and a young camel were roasted over great fires. They baked roots in the coals. After the feast, both the men and the women danced. Older hunters told stories of great hunts. Medicine men told their stories about demons. Everyone sang the songs of the tribe.

Suddenly the dogs started howling, integrating their voices with those of the humans. The singers stopped. The entire group stared at the animals. Ktoh and Dōshi seemed not to notice and continued their duet. The children joined the howling twosome. The youngest howled from fear. The older children howled in joy. All the adults broke into laughter. They stomped their feet and clapped their hands. No one got to bed easily that night.

The next new sun, when most of the people were still asleep, Ktoh started acting strangely. She circled her pen. She sniffed here and there almost in fear.

Dōshi joined her in her routes around the pen. He barked at this spot and yipped at that one. Finally, Dōshi chose a spot close to the bachelor lodge. He started to dig a hole. Ktoh stopped her search and joined him. When they got to the permafrost, both dogs started howling. Their howls were heard throughout the community.[i]

Nauja was the first to arrive. He didn't know what to do. He started to panic. Sacha joined him. Sacha was overjoyed as well as excited but was not the least bit concerned.

"Nauja, gathered caribou and moose antlers. We must build Ktoh a den," Sacha instructed.

"Why? What is happening Sacha? Why are they behaving like this?" Nauja demanded desperately.

"Mieto," laughed Sacha. I told you, they were mieto."

"I don't understand. I remember you telling me a word like that when you woke up. But you never explained. I thought it was the word for friends between dogs," Nauja responded worriedly.

"No, it means more than friends, it means…it means… joined mates. Ktoh is going to have puppies and she must have a den."

At this news, Nauja took off running. He stopped everyone he came to and pleaded for moose antlers. The women laughed in joy because they all knew that Ktoh was expecting pups. And they laughed at Nauja too. "Isn't it just like a man not to notice a woman's belly until it can't be ignored," they all said.

A proper den was built for Ktoh. Soft furs and sweet-smelling grasses covered its floor. They would protect against the cold permafrost. Nauja refused to leave Ktoh's side.

Many women died in childbirth. He wanted to be by Ktoh's side if she should walk the wind. He wanted to be the last thing she saw before walking the wind. And he wanted

---

[i] Dōshi's behavior is nearer to wolves than domesticated dogs. Since these dogs were biologically closer to wolves than our dogs today, their behavior regarding new puppies may have followed that of wolf packs.

h.c. Clarke

her soul to touch his own one last time so that they would never part.

The entire area was circled by women all wanting to hear when the puppies were born. It was always a great sun when a new life entered the world. This sun was different, special. This was the first time a new animal life entered the world. The group of women created a wind break around Ktoh's little den. Not a puff of cold air could get through.

Two hands plus three pups were born that sun. Dōshi, the proud father, stood guard at the entrance to the den. He allowed Nauja to be near but had chased him out of the actual den.

Ktoh was resting among the big litter. She licked each one. Nauja told Sacha that she looked beautiful. "I know I shouldn't describe a dog with a woman's trait, but she does. She is glowing with beauty."

Sacha laughed at Nauja. "You are a strange one, Nauja the Seagull. You truly are. I hope I can make a future mate as happy as Yuka will be with you. I don't know who looks prouder, you or Dōshi."

Three moons after the pups were born, Nauja and Sacha started to train them. They didn't tell the others that they had never trained their own dogs. Dōshi was given to Sacha already trained. Ktoh had trained Nauja. The pups had been named simply with numbers according to their sizes.

The tribe elders approached Nauja and Sacha. They begged the boys to remain. "You may choose any family. You may choose a family with high status. When you die, you will go to the pillar of your new family. The ancestors will be happy to have a new member. We have done this before; not often for we do not need more people, but for you…and um…your dogs, we would welcome you into The Pillars of the Ancestors."

Nauja looked at Sacha. He saw the signal they had agreed upon to mean a negative. He put his hand on the elder's upper arm. "Honorable Elder, we are grateful for your offer. But I'm afraid we must decline. We want to return to my tribe.

"Well, Nauja, I am sorry to hear your answer. We were so hoping to add your leadership to our own. We have seen that you would administrate fairly. Why don't you take a few suns to think about it? Did I mention that your dogs will be welcomed also? Into the tribe that is. And they will join the pillar of your chosen new family. The elders have all talked about it," the elder's assertion was surprising.

Nauja was confused. It was common for a tribe to welcome in a stranger. Sacha planned to join The People of Beringia as full member. But this repeated mention of the dogs confused him. "Thank you, Honorable Elder. But we do not need a few suns. Your kindness these dark moons has been greatly valued. But Sacha and I have already planned our trip back to my tribe."

Then he found out the real incentive for being invited to join the tribe. "Well, Nauja. If you are convinced that you will not stay, the elders have authorized me to offer a sufficient price for a pair of pups.

"We assure you that they will be given only to happy homes. We have planned a ritual to take them in as special members. They will be given their own pillar. Then they can watch over their kind for all time."

Nauja smiled and glanced over at Sacha again. Sacha nodded his head indicating that he concurred. "Honorable Elder," Nauja began. "We will not sell you any of the pups. We will give you one male and two females. You will be able to increase the size of your dog tribe. We hope this is payment enough for the generosi…....."

The elder was joyful. He turned and hurried as fast as his bent old legs could take him. He went back to the group of elders waiting for him. They talked and giggled among themselves. And they patted the back of the spokesman.

"I don't think they really wanted us," Sacha noted laughing. I think they just wanted the dogs. Now you gave them an outcome they could never have hoped for.

"Do you really think so, Sacha? They just wanted the dogs? Are the dogs that much of a prize?"

"Look at them, Nauja! They are cheering as if they had beaten death. They were determined to acquire dogs. They have seen how useful dogs are. Yes, I'm sure. You heard them. They rarely take in strangers to their tribe, but they would have taken us just to get the dogs.

"But they only wanted the dogs. I am sure that if we had refused both to stay and to sell them dogs, they would have stolen them. They would have claimed the dogs had just run off."

Nauja stared at Sacha. "If the dogs are that important to this large and wealthy tribe, might the dogs be the gift I am looking for? Might they be a useful finding for my own tribe?"

"Yes, Nauja! Of course! That's it! The DOGS. Your gift has been with you all along. The dogs will be a wonderful gift, the perfect gift, the best of all gifts."

Nauja was relieved. He felt a physical weight fall from his body. "But, Sacha, we will keep all the pups that have two different eye colors. They are the special ones."

The boys asked for three people to learn how to train the dogs. There were more volunteers than they dreamed. They chose carefully. It was important that the new owners should love their animals.

They chose two young men and one woman. They trained these new owners along with the pups. This way the new owners learned the methods to train more in the future.

The elders were marking their success in gaining dogs. Nauja was rejoicing in finding his gift. It seemed that all was right with the world. But sorrow can come without warning.

Chapter 14

Nunyae

A strong woman knows she has the strength for the journey, but a woman of strength knows it is the journey where she will be strong. That night, Nauja, Sacha, and the other young men were wakened by the sound of weeping. A young man started rubbing himself with ash. He started a softer wailing.

"He is the brother of the young woman whose child walked the wind tonight. The ash will identify him as a family member." The death of an old man or woman was celebrated, but the death of a child was a loss felt by the whole tribe.

Women came from each of the huts to participate**Error! Bookmark not defined.** in the sad chant and to support the mother. As one woman tired, another took her place. There were never fewer than both hands of women joining in the sad song. The men took out their tools and started carving.

The carvings depicted people and animals, to the best of the men's recollections. The figures did not need to be elaborate. Even the simple carvings of young boys were allowed. It was their duty to provide guides so that the baby would not be alone on his journey. The ancestors would be waiting for him.

Suddenly Ktoh began howling. She copied the sad tones of the women. Dōshi added his lower tones to the howl. Each pup joined in with the emotional cries of the women.

Just like the women when a dog was tired another took up the sound. Nauja had never in his life heard such sadness. It was as if the very earth were crying for the loss of this child.

h.c. Clarke

The women took the mother into the chief's lodge. They surrounded her and her dead baby and sang funereal chants. Meanwhile, the men went into the family's hut. They scraped away the cooking hearth. Then they dug through the dirt beneath.

The cooking fires had melted the ground below, but the ground was still frozen. They built another fire with pitch. This makes the fire burn hotter and melt the ground beneath. They repeated this many times until they reached the proper depth.

One woman from each hut brought a burning stick from her own hearth. The men brought the carvings they had made. When the fire was burning hot with coals, the mother and baby were brought to the hut.

They wrapped the baby tightly in the fur of a young animal. The father gently placed him on top of the hot coals. His head pointed to the west toward the pillars. They placed the sacred carvings on top of child and filled in the grave. They replaced the woman's cooking fire.[i]

Nauja thought the ceremony was beautiful. The mother had had time to hold her baby. Since it was just beneath her cooking hearth, it would always be near her. She would make sure to keep her cooking hearth burning hot. This would keep her baby warm on its way to the ancestors.

After the moon cycle, she would check for a wind that made a whistling sound. This would be indicative of the baby's arrival and the joyfulness of the ancestors welcoming her child.

The dogs became part of the tribe that night. Everyone was amazed. These animals understood their customs and had helped the mother with her mourning song. It was talked about all through the dark moons.

Often when Nauja looked for Sacha, he couldn't find him anywhere. One time, Nauja found Sacha chatting with a

---

[i] Digging into an 11,500-year-old hearth in Alaska, archaeologists discovered the cremated remains of two infants.

young woman. They were so deep in their conversation that neither noticed Nauja, so he slunk away, leaving them alone.

Later that evening, Nauja teased Sacha. "I saw you with that young woman, Sacha. Have you changed your mind about fighting me for Yuka?"

One of their hut mates said, "Of the vast availability of young women, Sacha, you choose the one who is most outspoken. You could have any girl here. Girls always go for strangers."

"Although I don't understand it, I suppose the rest of us should be relieved that you choose the one none of us wants."

Sacha blushed. "Yes, Nunyae is a beautiful young woman and very skilled. You should see the complexity of the designs she makes on her baskets.

Later, when they were alone, Sacha said to Nauja, "I tested your assumption that smart women are worthwhile."

"And what came of your test?"

"You saw for yourself what came of it, Nauja. I fell in love."

Nauja became serious. "Am I going to lose you, Sacha? Are you thinking about staying with this tribe? I will be very sad if you do not accompany me home, but I recognize that you are not from my tribe. You have no reason to go with me."

"Do not worry, Nauja. I will be returning with you. And you should be happy that I will not be fighting you for Yuka's hand. Nunyae is a strong woman just like your Yuka. You convinced me that a strong woman can be an equal life partner. Everyone has told me that Nunyae will not be chosen as a mate here. She is too outspoken. These people are like yours and mine. They do not like clever

h.c. Clarke

women. Nunyae will be coming with us."[i]

Nauja was surprised. "She is willing to leave her tribe? She is willing to give that up joining the pillar of her ancestors?"

"Yes, she is willing. She is my little wolverine," he said, referring to the meaning of her name. She never lets go of what she knows to be a truth. She knows she is judged too outspoken to be a good mate here. She wants a husband that sees her as a partner. And she is willing to immigrate to a place where she can have a friend like Yuka who won't scold her for speaking her mind."

Nauja felt homesick. Time couldn't pass fast enough. He had to control himself from being short with his hut mates whenever they spoke of their various young women. He had to force himself to be happy for Sacha, but this only made his unhappiness sharper. He had arguments with his own thoughts.

A good leader puts the needs of others ahead of his own.

But I am not a leader. I am the only son of a lowly flint knapper. Why do I feel that I need to act as a leader?

Because you are the alpha member of more than both hands of dogs and now three humans.

But I won't be when we get home!

But you are now. And your pack members, your people, depend on you now.

When the ice began to melt and the rivers were full, Sacha grew as restless as Nauja. They wanted to be on their way. The elders seemed happy to have her go. A single female was generally a burden to both her family and the tribe in general.

When Sacha approached Nunyae's father, he agreed to let her go. But he insisted that they be joined before they

---

[i] Siberia attracted a lot of genetically distinct peoples, and they interbred widely until about 25,000 years ago.

leave. "I will not bring shame on my family by letting her go off without a mate," her father had said.

The joining ceremony was held the next sun and Sacha and Nunyae moved into their own hut. There had not been much fanfare because it was too early to hold the joinings of others which would happen in The Moon When Berries Ripen.

Nunyae packed her things and the many skins given to her as joining gifts to build a hut for a new family. Finally, the sun came when Nauja announced that they would leave for Beringia the next new sun.

That night when Nauja was sleeping, a scream pierced the world. A cat's scream. It pierced water, pierced rocks. Rocks and water were battling each other in a war of elements. Nauja saw Ktoh swimming. Swimming for him. The water was spinning and spiraling, twisting and twirling. The earth was fighting back. Rocks were rolling, splashing, tumbling. The battle wore on, the battle between earth and water, and Ktoh was in the middle of it.

Ktoh's legs worked harder, all four of them pumping, swimming. She ignored the swirling, spinning rocks, but something was holding her back. She strained, she growled, she bit. Her head went beneath the water. He cried at her death, adding his tears to the churning water.

Chapter 15

The Trip Home

We will be known forever by the tracks we leave.

Nauja woke up sweating in fear. He'd been dreaming, but what was the dream about? He couldn't remember. A fear caught him; what if it wasn't a dream but a vision?

If he couldn't remember the vision, how could he use it to help himself and his friends? He left the hut, the night still upon them. He looked up at the stars and put his hand over the scar on his chest and begged. "Help me blue star. Help me to remember the vision so that I can help my friends."

A panther's scream broke through the silence of the early new sun and the dogs began to howl. A rock fell from the sky, and it started to rain. He remembered that rocks and water were in his vision. Rocks, water, a cat, and the dogs. They were all in the vision, but what did it mean?

The first rays of the sun started to peek over the mountains. His friends found him sitting cross-legged on the ground. He was in a deep trance, looking toward the stars.

Their new friends had drawn many maps in the dust to show them a route as far east as they knew. An orphan boy from the tribe was going to go with them. The young boy was curious about the world. They gave him permission to find new things, new customs, new knowledge.

The puppies had been trained to wear a harness and pull a sledge. They had also learned to cull out a single animal from a herd. Remembering Sacha's report of people eating the dogs, Nauja made it clear that the dogs should never be used for food.

They had demonstrated how the dogs improved the lives of the people. They had shown the people how the dogs helped in hunting. And how they added protection to everyone in the tribe. It would not be wise to eat them, even during starving times. The dogs should be thought of as valuable members of the tribe.

The young orphan, Miru, was excited. He could hardly control his anticipation of being a world traveler. He wanted to be like Nauja and Sacha. He was as outgoing as Sacha. His help on the trip would be useful. Nauja felt a fleeting sense of envy. *I am glad to have time for my own thoughts, but I have already lost part of my friend to Nunyae. Am I going to lose more to this chatty young boy?*

Ktoh and Dōshi pulled their sledge in front. The other five pairs of pups followed. Nauja was a little worried. "Sacha, do you think we have gone beyond the capacity of the sledges? Does Nunyae genuinely need all that she has packed?"

"I don't know. Nauja, you're the one that said women are as smart as men. I'm certainly not going to challenge her on it! I'm sure she will have a justification for everything she's taking. Would you tell *Yuka* to leave behind what she felt she needed?" Sacha argued.

"No. You are right. OK, let's see how it goes. If the dogs strain will have to think of an alternative. We could increase the capacity of our own packs."

Nauja watched the pups. He wanted to see if he could establish which of them would show the touching of souls he had with Ktoh. Nunyae was close with Treenat. The dog would not leave her side unless it was being harnessed to a sledge. The young dog had different colored eyes. Nunyae showed fear when Nauja tried to convey his theory. This was a clue that their souls had touched. Nunyae watched over Treenat carefully. So much so that often Sacha became jealous of the dog.

The following suns were filled with travel over rough mountainous terrain. Just walking took all their energy. They only talked in front of the fire each evening. Nauja generally talked about his tribe and their traditions.

They planned their introduction to the tribe. Nauja wanted it to be perfect. He had made small changes he hoped would not be noticed. They practiced it every evening for the

h.c. Clarke

entire trip home.

With Miru and Nunyae along, they could not maintain the distance he and Sacha would have been able to cover by themselves. It was also a much bigger process to unpack five dragging sledges instead of just one.

"Tomorrow, let's take a sun of rest. We need to repack all the sledges. One sledge should have what we need on a nightly basis. We will obviously need Nunyae's tent and sleeping furs for Miru and me. What else?" asked Nauja

Nunyae's tent and its support branches was a load all by itself. This sledge also carried the six other branches that they would add to the tripod for extra support to hold the heavy skins.

It was just for their trip. The hides would be used for her hut once they arrived. The frame was a bundle of branches tied at the top. It was only as high as Nunyae herself, but it took all three boys to wrap the skins over the frame.

They would not arrive at the lands of the Beringian people until just before the dark season. They walked as long as the sun still gave them light. They wanted to avoid getting caught by the endless night.

They spent several nights with a tribe along the way. The dogs needed rest. Nunyae enjoyed chatting with other women. They traded one female and one male dog for meat, so they would not want to stop to hunt. The elders wanted to purchase another female, but Nauja felt he could not spare another.

"I will try to return with more pups, or Miru will bring some when he goes back to his own tribe," Nauja promised.

The second tribe they visited was where Nauja's father had spent the dark moons on his own manhood trek. Nauja's mother had been from this tribe. Nauja met members of his Mother's family.

Because of this they were treated like family. Nauja avoided telling them that his mother was considered crazy or that his father had the lowest rank.

The tribe knew they had delayed the little group. They told them of a pass through the mountains that would cut a lot of time from their trip. This made the stay worthwhile.

Nauja enjoyed the visits but worried over the loss of four more pups. Here, they traded another pair of dogs for an additional hide cooking pot, meat, and roots.

Sacha pointed out that Ktoh was going to have more pups. "Now you have made me worried. Pulling the big drag sledge is too much for her, Sacha," Nauja cried.

He tried to harness her to a smaller sledge, but Ktoh and Dōshi refused to move. Both Sacha and Miru laughed at him. But Nunyae understood his love for Ktoh. She told him that exercise is good for women who were with child.

"When my tribe was on a long hunting trip, even the women carrying babies in their bellies accompanied the hunters. And they carried large bundles on their backs as well."

"But those are people," Nauja argued. "And they did not pull great dragging sledges."

"And Ktoh is a wild thing, Nauja. Are you telling me wild things have to be more careful than people? I truly wonder how you got this far on your own," Nunyae laughed.

"I envy this Yuka of yours. She will have an easy life if you feel you need to pamper a woman with child. Women are strong. That's why they were chosen to give birth to babies.

"People would die out if men had to carry the next generation in their bodies." She was not yet ready to tell the small group that she thought she was carrying a babe of her own in her belly.

"You will like my Yuka, Nunyae. You are like her. You speak your mind."

Yes, Nunyae was like Yuka, Nauja thought. *The way she laughed at him. The other girls in the tribe would never dare to laugh at a man. They would giggle together when no man*

h.c. Clarke

was about, but never in front of the men.

"Yes, I think I will," Nunyae replied. "Sacha has told me all that you have told him. I am sure we will be great friends. We must plan our huts close together. Then we can share in the work as if we are one big family."

"What about me?" Miru chimed in. "I need to be part of your family."

"When you are old enough to take a mate, you can build your hut with ours," Nunyae assured him. "You must choose a woman who is not afraid of men. A woman who will speak her mind.," she added. "When Sacha told me of Nauja's Yuka I knew I wanted to meet her. I wanted to be part of her tribe. I don't think I will miss the girls or women of The Ancestors in the least."

"But won't you be sad not to join your ancestors?" Sacha asked worriedly.

"No. I don't think so. I will be just as happy watching my grandchildren from the stars above."

Chapter 16
Miru
Children learn from what they see. Set an example of truth.

"But I do not want a mate," Miru cried. "I do not want a woman to boss me around. I want to be free to go and do as I please."

"It is good that you do not want a mate," Nunyae replied. "You are too young for one anyway. No woman would take you for a husband; certainly not one like Yuka or me,"

Sacha laughed loudly. "You have time yet to decide, Miru," said Sacha between his bursts of laughter.

"I have the perfect woman in mind for you, Miru," Nauja added. Yuka has a younger friend. She is probably her only friend. This girl is strong in her own way but rarely speaks at all. She shows her strength by staying close to show her support. No one would guess that she is as strong as she is, but I happen to know that she is friends with Yuka in defiance of her own parents.

"And she will be a good contrast to your chattiness. When we get home, I will ask Yuka to put in a good word for you to Oomsa."

Miru did not like to be the cause of everyone's laughter. "I will not need a manhood trek. I have already journeyed with you."

"Your manhood journey must be alone for at least two moons, Miru. This way the People will know you are able to feed yourself. Then you will be able to feed the tribe.

If you choose not to stay, you will have to make the trek back to your own tribe alone. Sacha and I will be staying put. We have travelled enough, isn't that right Sacha?"

"I agree," Sacha chimed in. "I've travelled enough for one lifetime, maybe even two, if we get another as the tribes to the south believe. Nor do I have the desire to return to my own people; Nunyae would not be happy there. I promised her family I would always try to make her happy. That will make me happy. It's a win/win situation."

Miru became contradictory. "Maybe a young man on his own trek will come with me back to my tribe. I will have had experience. That will be my trek. Since I will be the leader, I will be like you, Leader Nauja. Being the leader is just like being alone."

Nauja stopped laughing. "I was totally alone for the requisite two moons, Miru. Do not worry, Miru. When we get home, you will live with me. My mother will make sure you are ready for a trek of your own or a return to your own tribe if that is what you want.

You are still young. A trip such as Sacha and I have been on is very frightening at your age. I was scared, but Mother made sure I was ready. You will be ready too. There is no reason to worry about it now."

Oh yes, she will make sure you are ready. You have much pain ahead of you my young friend, Nauja thought to himself.

Miru turned his head away. Nauja recognized the move. Miru did not want them to see the tear he was wiping from his eye. Nauja turned away and as he did so, he saw Sacha turn away also. A man deserved a quiet moment to control a tear or two.

Boys were taught that they should not show weakness. That was why he liked Yuka so much. In his Last Childhood Season, Yuka had led him behind a hut away from the boys who had been teasing him. Now, many cycles later, he did not remember the reason, only the result.

She had said to him, "Nauja, I know you are upset at what the other boys are saying. They are bullies. Soon you will not give them the power to affect you, but that time is not now.

And I know that this sun you do not want to cry in front of them. They will only laugh the harder. I had to pull you away so that you can let your tears fall in a safe place. I will never tell anyone that I have seen you cry."

Nauja remembered the tears falling down his cheeks and his hateful retort, "Go away! Leave me alone!"

Yuka had spoken softly again. "You think you want to be alone, but I know you really do not. It is always better to have a friend sit quietly by your side when you are sad." Then she remained quiet, sitting beside him.

When his tears had stopped, Yuka had told him a funny story about the tantrum one of the other boys had had during spear practice. The boy had missed the target, and his spear had broken when it flew into a rock. He had blamed the rock for being too hard and breaking his spear point. The boy had begged his father to throw the rock into the sea as punishment! That story had made them both laugh, helping Nauja regain his self-control and return to the group of boys.

Nauja's thoughts returned to his tribe. He realized how much he missed home. He missed his parents and Old Átenaq. He missed his best friend, Raven. And he especially missed Yuka. A tear of his own threatened to fall from his eyes.

A tear of his own threatened to fall from his eyes, so he focused on the memory of how he and Yuka had laughed. A rock could not take revenge for being speared.

I am sure that Nunyae and Yuka will like each other. They are so much alike. I am not as sure that Sacha and Raven will get along.

He remembered the words of Old Átenaq at the dawn of his challenge. "I know he has been your friend. He defended you against the others. But did you never notice *when* he stepped in?"

He wasn't sure if Raven liked him for himself. It might be that Raven gained attention for being nice to a low-born. He knew that Sacha liked him for himself.

They had argued on this long trip. It was normal that people argue once in a while. With Sacha he could share moments without fear of being mocked.

And Sacha could do the same. They would listen to each other's opinions. And when they listened, they truly listened. Each gave all of his attention to the other.

Nauja chuckled to himself. He remembered the moment he

had discovered Sacha's *tell;* a signal that showed Sacha when his mind was being changed.

Sacha would first scratch behind his ear. Then he moved his finger down his jaw until his chin. Nauja had never told Sacha that he saw this tell. It would not be wise to let a man know you could read his thoughts.

He had learned about the tell when Sacha had been teasing him about his long eyes. Nauja had replied, "Well, you'd better be careful with those big round eyes of yours. You will be mistaken for a caribou. You may find a spear flung your way."

"At least I don't have to worry about finding a gift when I don't know what to look for. I can't imagine a man's status would rely on what he can give to the tribe," Sacha had replied.

"I'd rather be judged on my own successes than on the luck of birth. In my tribe, a man gains through his own work. And each man has an equal opportunity to advance."

That is when Sacha put his hand behind his ear, rubbed gently, and followed it down his jaw almost to his chin. Nauja had recognized that movement. He had seen Sacha do it before. Nauja realized Sacha made this same action when he was thinking deeply. And each time, Sacha had changed his mind about something.

Ktoh's growl prevented any more pondering. Her growl was a low purring. The danger growl was one with threat to it. Sacha knew the growl too, as did Dōshi responding with his own, "get me out of this harness" growl. The six remaining pups answered their parents with their own squeals and yips of excitement.

As Nauja, Sacha, and Miru released each dog, it sat stone still. Each whimpered with the waiting as if they were saying, "Hurry up. We want to chase; we want to herd." The moment the last one was unharnessed they all took off together at top speed.

Nauja and Sacha always marveled at how each dog seemed to know precisely when to start running. Each had a role to play and knew what to do.

Ktoh chose the target and started to separate it from the herd. Dōshi was right by her side.

The pups took care of distracting the main herd. They kept the herd away from the target. Dōshi and Ktoh herded the lone caribou farther away from the herd.

This time, knowing they had the pups to help, they had chosen a nice fat young stag. Because it wasn't a calf, the major part of the herd wasn't fixed on defending it.

The pups forced the herd to give up on the buck. Ktoh and Dōshi confused and harried the young male heading him straight back to where Nauja, Sacha, and Miru were running toward them.

All three spears flew through the air. Nauja and Sacha had given a quick nod to each other and had held back a tiny bit. This gave the boy the first chance at the kill. It would mean so much to him. They were rewarded for their kindness when they heard Miru's happy cry of joy.

"HOORAH! It was **mine**! **I** killed it. I beat **both** of you. Take **that** you two. You can't call me a child now. HOORAH! HOORAH! I killed it."

Miru gained back his self-control and returned to his outgoing self. Everyone spent the rest of the light skinning and butchering. They tossed this or that piece to each of the dogs. Everyone was happy.

h.c. Clarke

Chapter 17
The Mother's Warning

The earth is our Mother. She nourishes us.

The little group continued on its way. The remaining journey was not uneventful. Late one evening, he dogs were sleeping; their brains still aware of the world around them. Dogs have a need to keep watch over their humans. The young people talked quietly amongst themselves…waiting.

The wolf pack watched the people. The people were unloading sledges, setting up the shelter, and starting a fire. The pack had been following the group. The pack wasn't very hungry. But the smell of the caribou was just too good to ignore.

The lead wolf thought it would be an easy steal. The group of humans was small, and they had not quite settled for the night. Also, the fire was small and contained in a circle of rocks.

But he also saw that the people were prepared. They had been warned by their slave dogs. They saw the humans all standing at the border of their campsite, spears ready. The leader had decided not to go after the humans. But a slave-dog disobeyed its master. It attacked his pack. A fight followed.

"Leave them to fight it out," the leader said to the other wolves. They had no fear of this weak young dog-slave. Three of the younger wolves disobeyed the leader and rushed in to join the fight.

It took every ounce of focus the other pups had to obey the strong "NO! STAY!" from Nauja and Sacha who were also yelling at Piŋa to return. Despite the mayhem, it was over soon. Nauja, Sacha, and Miru had thrown their spears. The end result was the death of one puppy and the wolf he had attacked. The other three wolves that had joined later also lay dead with spears in their bellies. The remaining wolves left.

The boys skinned the four wolves. They left the bodies of the wolves where they lay but buried the foolish puppy. They wrapped him in the skin of the wolf he had killed.

"This may give him comfort for his journey ahead," Nunyae said. "He did what he thought was right. He thought he was protecting us. He earned this pelt for himself."

They left early the next new sun. No one wanted to stay near the skinned bodies of the four unburied wolves. Their meat would be left for scavengers. Meat eating animals were not eaten by people.

They continued up the banks of the small river. It was flowing through a mountain pass. They had been told that the river never entered a canyon. They would be able to follow it all the way through to the eastern side of the mountains.

Dōshi pulled his own sledge. Ktoh was harnessed with Ata, the largest male pup. Neither of them liked this arrangement, but Ktoh nipped at Dōshi to herd him to the single-dog sledge. Nauja had made her realize the necessity for the change.

The hand plus two remaining dogs kept them in fresh meat. They feasted on the rich hump of camel and sheep. They added the skins to the growing pile on the sledges.

The suns began to blend into each other. The excitement of their journey was gone. They each carried heavy packs on their backs and plodded behind the sledges. There was no talk or laughter at the campfire. They cooked, set up the tent, and fell asleep.

It was a cold, sunny morning. After high-sun, they rounded a bend in the river to find, staring them in the face, a huge spear-toothed cat poised for attack. Its head was all jaws. Vicious fangs protruded from its mouth, saliva dripping. The look on its face was deadly.

Nunyae said, "It has cubs. Only a cat with cubs could look that angry. We've walked into its den. One of us will be joining the ancestors this sun."

Suddenly, all the dogs started snarling and pulled at their harnesses. They wanted to be let loose to fight this great beast and protect the lives of the people. But they never got the chance to fight. Neither did the cat.

Birds of every kind flew into the air. It looked like they were all part of one great flock. They cast a huge shadow over the showdown between the people and cat below. Even the mostly flightless birds took to the air.

Next came every other small animal that lived in the area. They were running for their lives. Nauja, Sacha, Nunyae and Miru stood frozen. They watched the strange scene. Other animals too had started to run. There were sheep, antelope, camel and steppe horses,[i] and even giant beavers.

The dogs started to growl and strain at their harnesses. They wanted to join the escaping mass. They would have taken off, but they had their humans to protect.

The great cat stood its ground. "It cannot leave without its cubs. They are probably in a hidden den, too young to move on their own," said Nunyae.

Nauja and Sacha directed the dogs toward the mountains on the other side of the river. They wanted to get out of the

---

[i] Once extinct in the wild, the steppe horse was reintroduced to Mongolia in the 1990s.

way of the stampede. But the dogs headed away from the cliffs. The young people had no choice but to follow.

"My vision," shouted Nauja. "The scream of a cat, rocks tumbling, water swirling. Water swirling! Head for high ground," he yelled.

Moments later, the earth began to rumble. Rocks began tumbling down from the cliffs. The ground shook beneath them. The people huddled near the sledges. They covered their heads as dirt, dust, rocks, and boulders came plummeting down from the cliffs above them.

Then the water in the shallow river rose above its banks. It flowed right up to the group of young people. It inched at their feet and then their ankles. It rose to the knees of the dogs. The dogs didn't know whether to bark or howl. The water didn't care about the howling; it rose.

The young people clung to the sledges, unsure of what to do. None of them had experienced an earthquake before and had no idea how the ground and the river would react. The water didn't care that the young people were afraid; it rose. Swirling and churning, it topped the heavy sledges pulling them, the dogs and the people with it. And still, the water rose.

The young people hung on to the heavy sledges. The water didn't care if the sledges were heavy; it rose. The very ground beneath them liquified.[i] The air was filled with screeching animals, the churning of water, and the rumbling of the earth. The once shallow river was a flood of swirling angry water. The water still rose.

Nauja braved a look up. He saw a great slide of mud and ice plunging down from the cliffs above. Everything and everyone was swept down river.

---

[i] A 6.5 magnitude earthquake or bigger would cause solid surfaces along the banks of a river to turn into liquid according to Dr. Ronaldo Luna.

h.c. Clarke

They were hit by rocks from above and slammed against rocks below.

Their mouths filled with muddy, gritty water. Their noses were hit with the foul smell of sulfur and silt. It was a battle between earth and water, and they were caught in the middle of it.

Nauja was trying to swim to shore, pulling his sledge with him. He frantically searched for Ktoh and saw her head bobbing in the furious water. She was not trying to get to shore but to swim to him. His vision. The water seemed a living thing, and it was angry. When he could keep his head above the swells for more than just a gulp of air, Nauja searched for Sacha and the others.

"Star, you warned me but did not explain. I could not understand what you were saying. Please help my friends and the dogs!" Nauja pleaded in his brain. He let go of the sledge. He could not swim and hold on concurrently. The moment he let go, the heavy sledge knocked into him, sending him careening toward the shore, yet the current pulled him back. Then it was a battle of human strength and the river's undertow.

He was about to give up when the current released him. It was pushing him back upriver. The entire flow of the river reversed its direction.[i] Nauja was pushed and pummeled back where he had come from. His conscious brain wanted to give up, but his body refused. His arms still pulled; his legs still pumped until finally all went black.

When he awoke several hands of the sun later, the world had gone silent. He was lying on his side on the bank of the river. The water had retreated to its course. It was as if it were embarrassed for having left its course. What living things that hadn't run fast enough were dead. He lay there trying to determine if he were still alive or walking the wind himself.

Then he felt a cold wet nose on his cheek and a warm

---

[i] The Mississippi River reversed its flow after Hurricane Isaac in 2012. Although this backwards flow wasn't permanent, the river flowed faster backwards than it does forwards on average.

wet tongue massaging his face. "Ktoh! You live? Or are we walking the wind together?" Nauja weakly asked the animal licking his face. Ktoh whimpered first, then started shaking her body all over in delight that he was still alive.

Sacha came into view. "So, you decided to delay your wind walking, dear friend. I'm so glad. I don't think I could have led our band to your lands by myself, much less hand over your gift."

"Sacha! Is that you? You still live? And the others?" Nauja managed to croak out through his sore lungs and throat.

"Yes, all of us still live. We were not foolish enough to let go of the sledges and try to swim. I think Miru and Nunyae held on solely because they didn't know how to swim. I knew that if a boat floats, it is best to stay with it. I figured it would eventually pull me to the shore. And since there had been no great waterfalls, I wasn't too worried about plunging to my death.

You, however, my friend, seemed to want to play hero. The moment I had a chance to look around, I saw you let go of the sledge and try to swim for shore."

"I was sure you were going to walk the wind this sun. And you did, I might add. It worries me a little that you chose not to stay with the wind. Was it so bad?"

"Why do you say that, Sacha? Why do you say I walked the wind?" Nauja rasped.

"Because you were walking the wind when I pulled you out of the water."

"You should have seen him, Nauja. He knew exactly what to do!" cried Miru. He turned you on your side and thumped you on your back. You vomited up almost as much water as in the river. Sacha said that's why we lived, because you swallowed all of the water, so there wasn't enough to drown the rest of us."

Nunyae interrupted Miru to tell the rest of the story. "Then he opened your mouth. He saw you weren't breathing. He blew into your mouth to give you his own breath."

Miru took back the storytelling and blurted, "Then he pressed your belly to make sure all the water was out. But the scariest thing was he got mad at your heart for not beating. He thumped it HARD. And yelled at it to start again. I didn't think

98   *h.c. Clarke*

Sacha was capable of such anger."

Nunyae stole the story back again, "And he made Ktoh and all the pups lie down along your body on both sides to keep the dead-cold from filling your body. And it worked, because here you are. We cheated the wind. We wouldn't let it have you. I hope it won't take revenge on us."

"Sacha?" Nauja questioned. "How did you know to do all that?"

"You forget that I come from a sea loving people, my friend. Drownings are common. Sometimes the methods work. Most often they don't. But sometimes they do," Sacha replied humbly.

Ktoh whimpered and rubbed against Nauja. She was happy that he was alive. Dōshi and several of the pups had left Nauja's side. They were searching the area where they had last seen the she-cat. It was nowhere to be found. It had been swept away by the waters or buried under the mud slide[i].

Nunyae, the practical one, clapped her hands as if herding young children away from a hut, and started to take charge. She had compiled in her mind a list of things that must be done. "Find wood that is not soaked. We need a fire. I think we could all use a bowl of willow tea, and if these furs are not to rot, they must be spread out to dry in the sun. At least it's still sunny." She stood up, shook her furs free of loose dirt and pebbles and started directing the two young men to do their part.

When Nauja started to rise, she looked at him sternly and said, "Oh no, you don't. Not you. You must lie quietly. Ktoh," she called as if the dog understood her.

"Ktoh and Treenat, stay by Nauja's side. We can't take a chance that he should get cold and become sick. Sacha has made it clear that he will not be able to get us to the land of

---

[i] In 2015, the remains of two cave lion pups were found in Sakha, Russia undamaged, fur intact. Scientists believe they were crushed in a mud slide.

The Gift   99

the Berigians. I do not want to go back to The Ancestors. So Nauja, you will simply have to lie there and rest and stay warm."

They spent the rest of the sun unpacking all the sledges. They spread out everything that could be saved. It was a productive time for all but Nauja. When the twilight arrived, Nunyae's little tent was set up. And a leg of fresh antelope killed in the flood was roasting over the fire.

Nunyae picked new willow stems for tea. This would lower Nauja's fever. The earth shook only slightly one more time. No animals fled, no birds bothered to fly away, and the cat had not returned.

Chapter 18
The Gift

Once you've been on your own, then even among family, you are never really home.

When the air got cold and the nights long, Nauja started to recognize the territory. He realized they were in the last phase of their journey. They had left the mountains for the steppe-tundra. The ground was damper. They had had to turn north to avoid the great ice sheet. Now they were on the northern edge.

They had seen herds of mammoth, but only three hunters could not kill the great beasts despite having the dogs. They just weren't willing to chance it.

"Besides," Nauja insisted. "We have plenty of meat and we don't want to load the dogs with mammoth ribs and tusks."

The tribe had seen him coming. Nauja knew they would. The People did not know who was arriving, but they knew a trekker was on his way in. When the little caravan arrived, the people had lined up in two rows so that the sledges arrived at the main lodge through a gauntlet. At the end stood Old Átenaq, smiling broadly. As the little caravan progressed down the gauntlet, the people gasped and backed up.

Nauja heard one woman whisper to her man. "Nauja must have learned great powers on his trip. He can command wolves to pull his burdens." That gave Nauja the courage he needed for his speech. He was no longer anxious. He stopped in front of the chief. It was all he could do to keep from running up and hugging him. Instead, he gave one command, "SIT." All the dogs sat, ignoring all the people around them and looked only at Nauja, waiting for the next command.

"Honorable Átenaq, leader of the People of Beringia, this lowly son of your tribe has returned from his manhood trek. He requests re-entrance to the tribe of his birth." These were the ancient words. They had not changed since time began. Only the chief's name had changed.

"What have you brought us Nauja, son of our tribe? What technology or knowledge do you bring to us as proof of your worth?" These too, were ancient words of re- entry.

"First, Great Átenaq, the only leader I have known, I bring you two new members. One is an excellent hunter, Sacha of the Jōmon People. He is robust in body yet of peaceful nature. He has chosen to follow me and requests membership to our tribe." Sacha stepped forward. As they had practiced, he stood at Nauja's side. This surprised the audience. Nauja heard the whispers. "If this Sacha person with the round eyes and wavy brown hair was really following Nauja, he should have stood behind him."

Nauja ignored the murmurs. *Lead by example,* he reminded himself. *Demonstrate the desired behavior.* "The second is Nunyae of the Pillars of the Ancestors. She has chosen to follow the man Sacha and become his mate. She will potentially give us more children for our future." Nunyae walked forward and stood beside her mate.

More whispers followed, "Look where she stands. Why doesn't she stand behind her mate as is proper for a woman?"

Old Átenaq turned to Sacha and waved him forward. "Is this true Sacha of another tribe? Have you followed Nauja of your own free will?"

Sacha bowed lowly. This was the custom of his people. "Yes, Honorable Chief. I would be greatly honored to become one of you."

"I look forward to seeing your skills, friend Sacha." Then he turned to Nunyae. "Is it true, Nunyae of the Pillars? You follow Nauja willingly, free of exploitation, and you are joined with friend Sacha. You are leaving your own tribe permanently?"

Nunyae stepped forward. In an uncharacteristic manner, she bowed her head as Sacha had done. This showed her duty to her mate. Nauja bit his tongue, hoping Nunyae would keep her opinions to herself this one time. "Yes, Honorable

h.c. Clarke

Leader. This is my wish." Nauja had never heard Nunyae exhibit such an economy of words.

"You also are welcome, my daughter. Old Átenaq looked at Miru but spoke to Nauja, "You have someone else present?"

"Yes, my Chief. I have brought a young member from Nunyae's tribe. He is too young for a trek of his own. He wishes to visit and learn about our tribe that he may bring back knowledge to benefit his own people."

Old Átenaq beckoned to Miru. "This is true young man? Speak freely. You have come by your own free will?"

"Yes, Venerable Old Man. I am an orphan, so no parents were there to prohibit me from following the Great Leader Nauja. It is a big tribe, so the loss of one member is minor."

Miru was like other outgoing young boys. He started to chatter on. He had been told never to call Nauja his leader but had forgotten. Adding "great" in front of it caused murmurings in the crowd. Old Átenaq suppressed a smile. He interrupted the young boy.

"We, the People of Beringia, admire adventure in a young man. You are welcome. As long as you remain here, you will be treated as one of us."

Old Átenaq turned once again to Nauja. "Are these people the extent of your gift to the tribe, Nauja?" he said eyeing the animals sitting behind Nauja. "Please specify what new knowledge they have that makes them a worthy gift?"

"These people are not my gifts and accordingly do not warrant your judgment, my Chief," replied Nauja unfalteringly."

The crowd gasped. "He has the audacity to defy the chief?"

"How dare he contradict Old Átenaq," said someone from the crowd in a voice all could hear. The voice sounded familiar to Nauja's ears.

Nauja continued, "I merely present them to you first, less

they distract you from the most valuable thing…things that I bring."

The people in the crowd whispered among themselves again. "Is Nauja being flippant with Chief?"

"Does Nauja dare to tell Chief he is wrong?"

"Where did this attitude come from?"

"Nauja has changed. Nauja used to be a polite boy who knew his place," said the familiar voice.

"He is no more arrogant than you," countered someone.

"He has simply gained self-confidence which is the way it should be," added others.

"By all means, son Nauja. Present us with your gift before I get distracted by old age and desire to take a nap after all this prologue," Old Átenaq teased, a playful gleam in his eyes.

"I have five *dogs* to present to you." Nauja emphasized the word *dogs*. Then Nauja called to the older pups, "Ata, Talli, Shest, Syem, Kulit, COME." The five young dogs slipped from their halters and came, almost as one, to sit in front of Nauja and look directly into his eyes, their backs to the old chief.

There were distinct gasps and whisperings from the crowd. The people backed away from the fearsome animals. "What lack of respect these animals show. They turn their backs to the Chief," pressed the familiar voice from before.

"But look at the power Nauja has over them," another said.

"Nauja is big-headed to train these animals to look to him and not Grandfather," said the familiar voice.

Grandfather? Nauja wondered, realizing why the voice was so familiar. He ignored his alarming realization and continued, "As you can see, Honorable Átenaq, they obey commands. They have been trained in hunting, fetching, and protecting.

They can hear far better than a man can hear. They see much farther than a man can see. And they smell odors in the

h.c. Clarke

wind far earlier than we. Once you allocate them to owners, I can teach the handlers the commands to use. You have seen that they obey; they are also strongly loyal and will protect their masters and their master's kin.

"Dogs have been used by tribes from the south for many generations," Nauja continued. "They help in the hunt, they warn of danger, and can locate things by smell. They can find a lost child or prevent it from getting lost. I look forward to showing you all their countless skills, Great Leader, and how these skills can be employed for the benefit of the tribe.

"I will also have more when Ktoh gives birth to the pups she carries. But they will need time to grow and train. Once owners are assigned, Sacha and I will teach others to train the pups."

"What of the other three?" yelled the voice from the crowd.

Old Átenaq asked the same thing, "Why are you not giving the tribe all of the... what do you call them? Dogs?"

Nauja looked straight into the old man's eyes, causing more gasps from the crowd. *I must be brave and stand up for myself and my friends,* he reminded himself. "The large male you see still harnessed does not belong to me, Honorable Átenaq. Dōshi came from the south with Sacha. He is not mine to give."

"Why isn't your follower giving the tribe his animal?" called out the voice. If he is truly your follower..."

Old Átenaq waved his hand to stop the comments.

"And the other two?" the chief asked gently.

"The payment to the owner of the sire is the pup of his choice. Treenat was that pup, so she is not mine to give either. Sacha is also owed the pick of the prospective pups, but the rest are included in my gift."

"And the one with the white patches of fur?"

"Ktoh is wild-born, Honorable Chief. She came to me of her own free will, starving, with the wind calling her name. She stays with me by choice. I did not catch her, I did not trade for her, nor was she a gift to me, therefore, I do not own her. She shies from other humans, even those I have brought with me. She listens to no one. She cannot be commanded by anyone. She obeys my commands when she feels they are to my benefit but will disobey if she feels a command has no reason.

"Her pups will not be wild-born," Nauja continued. They will listen to their handlers *without question*," Nauja placed emphasis on the final words in order that no one should think the animals were not trustworthy.

Then he took a great risk, although he knew the right criteria existed. "It would please me, Honorable Átenaq, if you were to call Ata, the largest of the pups, to sit before you. Say the dog's name with the one word 'come.' That is all you should need to call him to you, and he will wait for your next instructions."

Old Átenaq looked at Nauja in disbelief. Call a wolf to do his bidding? But he had seen Nauja do it, and he could not refuse, whatever his personal fear of these fierce looking animals. Like the others of the community, he was not truly at ease with all of them amongst his people.

"Ata, COME," called old Átenaq. He spoke in a strong commanding voice to mask the fear he felt. Ata stood and turned to the chief as if deciding whether he would obey this strange voice. Everyone was holding their breath in anticipation.

h.c. Clarke

Chapter 19
Ata and Átenaq

Looking into the eyes of an animal, I see a friend and feel a soul.

The look Nauja saw on the old man's face showed that his soul was connecting with Ata's. The human and the animal held each other's gaze. Finally, a small whimper came from Ata. It was not a whimper of fear. It was a whimper of knowing.

Átenaq broke the gaze. He looked at Nauja with both fear and respect. He was feeling the same thing Nauja had felt when his soul had first touched Ktoh's. He was afraid of the connection. He was afraid of the power the two of them had together. This feeling of oneness with an animal was too new.

Nauja came to stand directly in front of the chief and bent low so others could not hear his words. And he used the term of endearment in place of the ceremonial title, "Do not be afraid, grandfather. I felt the same way when my soul first touched that of Ktoh's. It is alarming, but it is also soothing. Do not talk of it to others. They will not understand, and it will frighten them."

The crowd was whispering again. "Who does Nauja think he is that he speaks privately to the Chief to without asking?"

"Look how self-assured he is that he leans to Chief. He has become a leader of men as well as dogs."

Nauja stood straight again. He returned to his spot beside Sacha and Nunyae. He waited for the Chief to respond. The Chief addressed the people. "I accept your gifts Nauja. And if it turns out these … 'dogs' as you call them, are all that you claim them to be, you shall be one of my advisors. You shall be second only to my grandson Raven."

Nauja was stunned. He had hoped to increase his status but to be named Second-Advisor-To-Chief? Nauja remembered his argument to Sacha, "At least in my tribe, a man has an equal opportunity to gain favor, to increase his station. It is not the luck of birth, but the result of one's own labors that determines your station in life." Now it was a reality, it was true. By his own efforts, he had earned the third highest station in the tribe.

"Do you wish to pledge yourself Nauja, son of The People of Beringia?" said the chief bringing Nauja out of his own thoughts.

Nauja bowed his head, partly to hide the tear sliding down his cheek, and recited the age-old Pledge of Entrance,

"Honorable Leader, this man wants only to help you and the people of his birth. I, Nauja, son of Beringia, do affirm, before and in sight of all the people, that I will dedicate my efforts, and use all my talents and abilities to safeguard the security, the well-being, and the progress of The People of Beringia, and that I will be faithful and bear true allegiance to its continuance. Should I break my oath, I will submit myself to the people for the requisite punishment."

There was cheering, but Nauja saw that not all the people cheered. Not all the people were pleased. Old Átenaq spoke again, "Go now, Nauja, Second-Advisor-to-Chief. Return to the hut of your father. Take care of your followers. The man Sacha and his mate may occupy one of the guest huts.

"For now, find the dogs food and shelter as their needs require. You and I will find handlers for them at another time. However, I suggest you restrict their freedom at this time."

Nauja bowed his head and spoke to the chief, "May I request, Chief Átenaq, that Sacha and Nunyae be allowed a hut at the edge of the community if one is available? It is important that the dogs not be too close to many people."

"Yes, of course Nauja. I'm sure you realize that outer huts have a lower station. I should think you would prefer one with the status he deserves as follower to one of my advisors."

"I understand. But it is as you said, it is best that we restrict the freedom of the dogs. We will build a pen between two of the huts on the edge of the community."

"Very well," said Old Átenaq. "You have my permission to request a family living next to your father's hut to move to a guest hut."

"Thank you, Chief. Nauja turned to the pups and commanded them, calling each by name, "Harness." The pups returned to their stations and stood ready. But Treenat and Ata did not. Treenat lay on the ground, put her head on her outstretched paws and whimpered. Whispers were heard through the crowd. "See, he cannot really command these wild beasts; they are a danger to the people."

"See, he cannot really command these wild beasts. They are a danger to the people."

"Look, the small one bows before him as if pleading to a higher power."

Nauja looked down at the small dog, and said, "Treenat; Nunyae Go." Treenat yipped in delight literally bounced herself to sit before Nunyae.

Again, whispers were generated in the crowd. "See how fair-minded Nauja is. He sends the small one to its rightful owner to be commanded. He will make an excellent advisor-to-chief."

But other whispers exhibited the negativity of those who used to be higher in status than Nauja, "Look how he gives in to the desires of a mere beast. He will be weak; he will be an inadequate advisor. He will fail."

Ata remained seated before Átenaq, waiting for the chief's command. Nauja stifled a chuckle. "Honorable Leader," Nauja said, "Ata knows that you are now his master. You must give him the command. He will no longer obey anyone else unless you are injured. Repeat his name followed by the command 'down.'"

Old Átenaq stared at Ata in disbelief. But again, he could not show doubt or fear in front of the people. He repeated Nauja's command. "Ata, Down."

Ata gave Nauja a last look as if to say goodbye. He turned and licked the old man's hand and laid down at his side. He was now content to be at the service of this man. The old chief had not had time to pull his hand away before Ata licked it. He did not look at the dog, but his hand fell to his side and started to stroke the fur on the huge dog's back.

Then Nauja directed the dogs to the hut of Nauja's birth.

When they arrived, his mother and father were waiting. They had been standing at the edge of the crowd as their station had required. They had hurried back to their hut to prepare for Nauja and the animals. Yuka arrived shortly after.

Nauja smiled deep within himself. *Second only to Raven in status. I will gain Yuka as my mate.* He bowed his head slightly to his parents and then made his request. "May I keep Ktoh and two of the pups in the hut father? The others will be with Sacha and Nunyae. It will only be until Sacha and I can build an pen for them.

"If you are sure they are safe, Son. I don't have a choice, do I? You are now the head of our family unit," his father responded, pride in his voice.

As soon as he finished his sentence, one of the neighbors stepped forward.

"Nauja, Advisor-to-Chief," the man spoke up. He used Nauja's new title. "My family is willing to move to the guest hut."

I'll bet you are, thought Nauja. The man was one of those who had whispered against him in the crowd. It would be a great honor for him to move closer to the inner circle. *I shall show him I am worthy of my title by not holding a grudge.* "Thank you, neighbor. Your kindness is greatly valued. I realize the trouble I am causing you," Nauja replied.

The next new sun, Nauja, Sacha and Miru built a pen with a hut for Ktoh. Raven and his cousin Kanik watched, sneering. After inspecting its construction to determine if it were appropriately built, Ktoh turned around three times and lay down on the furs inside her hut.

"It seems that your little den is adequate, Ktoh. Now you will have a den when your time comes."

Shortly after first entering her den, Ktoh gave birth to a hand plus one pup. When they heard the fuss, Raven and Kanik came back to see what was going on. Raven looked over the pen and was met with fierce teeth and threatening growls.

Chapter 20

A Change in the Wind

Between who you once were and who you are now becoming, is where the dance of life really takes place.

Despite all the watching people, Kanik yelled angrily, "You would bring wolves into the tribe, Nauja? I do not understand. Have they converted you to their pack? Have you become a wolf because you knew you could never become a man? Are you seeking payback on your betters? You bring killers into the tribe and call it a gift? You have become crazier than your mother!"

Kanik's words did not bother him the way they used to. He realized Kanik was just a bully. He was trying to impress his own betters by putting down someone else.

Nauja explained in a tone used with children, "You will understand, Kanik, when I have demonstrated their skills. They are not wolves, they are dogs. Many tribes to the far south of us use these dogs. They are well-known and prized for their talents. You should not be so quick to judge what you do not understand, Kanik."

Raven looked at Nauja in shock. To scold a man of higher status was unheard of. And to do it in front of others was worse. He leaned close and whispered, "Nauja, do not be so rude. Kanik is a valued member of the tribe. Remember Nauja, he is my cousin, grandson of Old Átenaq's brother! Be careful with your words."

Nauja's response was calm but angry. "He calls my mother crazy-woman, yet you expect me to be respectful. Respect must be mutual, Raven. It must be earned through deeds not birth. But I will be the bigger man." He turned to Kanik and spoke as if he were speaking to a child. "I'm sorry, Kanik, if you found my words offensive."

This was one of the strategies he had learned from Sacha.

Sacha called it a "non-apology." You say you are sorry that a person feels a certain way. But you do not say you are sorry for saying the words that caused those feelings. "Many times," Sacha had said, "it allows both parties to save face. An apology is made but does not show regret for the offense that caused it."

Kanik did not know how to respond. Nauja seemed to be saying he was sorry. But Kanik did not hear shame in Nauja's voice. Kanik just nodded his head in acceptance. He wanted to add more bitter words but felt they would be received as bitter for no reason.

Raven was amazed at the self-confidence Nauja showed. *Where is the meek boy they had all enjoyed teasing? This youth is not like the Nauja I remember. Even the way he stands seems different. Is he taller?* Raven thought to himself.

Sacha whispered under his breath, "Atta boy. You go Nauja!" To Nunyae and Miru, standing close to him, he said, "He has made a fool out of the one who attempted to make a fool out of *him*. Hah!"

"Shhh," hissed Nunyae.

But Sacha was enjoying the scene too much to let it go. "Nauja has become the leader I knew he would be. I'm proud to be following him."

The next suns were busy ones for Nauja. He and Sacha were eager to demonstrate how useful the dogs were. The dogs picked out one animal from the herd, leading it right to the hunters. The hunters were awed at the skills of the dogs. They found the hunt was much easier.

A few tried to claim the hunt was not as fun. They claimed the hunt did not show off the skills of men. These were laughed at by the rest. This did not improve the views of those who had complained.

Nauja and Old Átenaq met many times to find suitable handlers for the dogs. A blend of gentleness and power needed to be found in each handler. Most of the people felt these factors could not exist together. But Nauja insisted that those chosen as handlers must be people who would love and respect their animals for the partners they could be. When

h.c. Clarke

they asked for volunteers, they included women, because one of the dogs would be assigned to women's tasks.

They chose carefully. Nauja insisted that those chosen must love and respect their animal. Someone who would see the dog as a partner. A handler could not give a dog's care to another family member. One of the men said he did not want to be a handler if he had to clean up after his dog, so they chose someone else.

If handlers did not live at the edge of the community, they were forced to trade huts with a family that did. Two handlers would live side by side with a pen and small dog hut built between the human's huts. This way, two dogs would live together.

At first, each handler who lived in the inner circle whined about being moved to the outer edges. Outer huts were lower in status. Soon, the women in the marginal huts began to enjoy a greater freedom. Neighbors did not snoop on them.

An outer hut became more prized. The inner huts began to lose status. The infrastructure of the community was changing.

Nauja began to get requests for the new puppies. Men of high status complained to Nauja. They said only important people should be chosen as handlers. They complained that the first handlers should have been chosen from those with higher stations.

Nauja always answered with the same words. "Chief Átenaq will decide based on an even-tempered nature. He also wants handlers to be fair, and be able to relate to animals. The dogs are not to be exploited."

"What do those aspects have to do with anything. I have greater status than those you chose in the first group. I should have been given a dog. You watch yourself, Nauja. We shall see who controls the wolf-dogs," some replied.

"I will remember this conversation," Nauja replied politely. *Oh yes, I will remember. This man will never be given a dog. He cares more about his own standing than the welfare of the dog. And he thinks bullying will get him his way*.

Others grumbled about a dog being named to women's tasks. "Dogs should only be given to hunters, Nauja. Some of us do not understand why you would give these valuable animals to women," whined a friend of Raven's.

"Lessening their tasks gives women more time to spend on treating hides and other chores that we men do not wish to do. In the end, it helps men also," Nauja replied calmly.

Nunyae demonstrated to the women how dogs could lessen their chores. Her dog could find the roots Nunyae liked. Treenat would yip and scratch the ground when she found one. As soon as Nunyae arrived at the spot, Treenat would race off to find another, leaving Nunyae to dig up each root properly without ruining its skin. It would stay fresher far longer if dug up carefully.

Then Nunyae left the dog in charge of three small children. Treenat kept the three close to each other. Each time a child started to wander, Treenat grabbed the child's tunic and dragged it back to the others.

Basically, the women didn't care about finding plants. They were curious about the animals. Nauja had gained status by bringing them. They thought being around the dogs might bring status to themselves as well.

Then Nunyae left Treenat in charge of three small children. The women hid so they could watch the dog and children interact. Treenat kept the three children close to each other. The small dog even grabbed a child's tunic if it started to stray. This ability interested the women more than the dogs' skill in locating plants.

Nauja's mother loved Treenat's ability to discriminate between similar plants. The animal invariably found them faster than any of the women. She taught Nunyae about the other plants and their uses, plants that were unfamiliar to the girl.

Yuka helped with Nunyae's education. She even taught Nauja's mother other ways to use the plants that Yuka had discovered on her own.

Nauja's mother had come to respect Yuka's ability to see new uses for plants. They had become good friends. When they saw Oomsa hanging about, they invited her into their group. Oomsa's broad smile was all they needed in return.

The suns became shorter and shorter and the nights colder and colder. Soon the endless night arrived, and the dogs proved their worth even more. More than once they growled a warning at approaching predators, making the entire community feel safer.

The long dark moons passed without a single hunter dying from an accident. Disease or old age were the only killers that season. No hunter was hurt if he was with a dog. Nauja's standing grew during the long dark season.

Sacha did not take part in many of the hunts. He would not tell Nauja why. Whatever it was, it required Dōshi harnessed to a sturdy sledge. The two of them would be gone until deep dark.

"What in the world are you doing, Sacha. You take off with an empty sledge but never bring anything back."

"It's a surprise," Sacha said.

One sun a woman started screaming in fear. All the people came running to find out what was the matter. On his way, Nauja heard many accusations.

"I'll bet a dog attacked the woman."

"Let us wait and see. You will prompt a riot," argued one of Nauja's supporters. But those who wanted to bring the young man down were louder than the others.

"No, I think it attacked her child."

"Did you hear? Two children have been attacked by two of those evil animals," cried another. Each time the rumor was repeated, it became worse.

As he ran to the screaming woman, Nauja hoped that the fight was not dog related. Even one accident including a dog would turn the people against them.

When he arrived at the scene, a circle of women surrounded another who was tearing at her clothes and hair.

"She was right here, I turned just for a moment and then

she was gone. Someone or something has taken her," the woman shrieked.

Sacha had also arrived on the scene followed by Dōshi. "Dōshi," he commanded. "FIND." Dōshi ran off away from the crowd. Sever women started screaming, "There he is, there's the evil one that took your daughter!"

h.c. Clarke

Chapter 21
The Ceremony

**Choose to listen to your inner voice,
not to the random opinions of others.**

When the men arrived, Dōshi was in a fight with a wolf. The child sat to the side screaming and crying but not hurt. The mother ran in to rescue her daughter. The men raised their spears towards the animals.

One man yelled, "Wait, we cannot hit one without hitting the other." Another man threw his spear yelling, "It does not matter, they are both wild and dangerous."

Sacha had expected this reaction. He threw himself at the man just in time to cause the spear to sail wildly away from the fighting animals.

"Dōshi has found and saved the child. He is not a wild animal. He was not wild-born. Leave him to fight the wolf. We shall see who wins."

This idea appealed to the men. They put down their spears. "We can always kill the winner if we choose," one man said. "I'll put a sheep's skin on the wolf, will anyone take my bet?"

"I will," replied Sacha. "But make it two!"

"Ha ha" laughed the man. "Foolish stranger. Look at the size of that wolf."

Many of the other men bet on one. Sacha matched each and every bet against Dōshi. The men did not know that Dōshi had fought a cave lion.

Sacha gained his own status. He became rich that sun. He won many skins. But the praise and respect he had gained was most important. Tired Dōshi dragged the wolf's body and dropped it in front of the child's mother.

"He is giving you the body of your child's attacker,"

Sacha said calmly. You may take revenge upon it."

The woman looked at Sacha. She turned and grabbed her husband's spear, driving it into the body of the great wolf. She picked up her child but turned once more to the dead animal and spat on it. Then she silently returned to her own hut.

The suns started to become longer. The promise of warmer suns to come calmed bad tempers caused by the long dark nights. The people started to prepare for the Choosing-of-Mates ceremony.

They held many hunts. The tribe believed that the number of diverse kinds of meat at the ceremony would determine the success of the pairings. Women were busy handling ducks, geese, and other birds. Hunters searched for caribou, musk ox, camel, giant beaver, and mammoth.

The matches were guaranteed to be successful if they killed a mammoth. It was a bad sign if a hunter was killed on any of the feast hunts. One year everything was cancelled because three young men were killed. They were to be joined that year.

The hunters were always careful on the mating hunts. But this year, they had dogs. No hunter was lost. There were more different meats than anyone could remember.

The women worked hard on new clothes and finery. They worked to produce the softest, most beautiful leather. They sewed beads of clay and bone onto leggings and tunics.

The ceremony was not needed for many couples. This was the case for Sacha and Nunyae. They had already joined in her own tribe. And they already had a baby.

Nauja was certain that Yuka would accept him. But Raven had been attending to all of Yuka's needs when Nauja was not around. Nauja began to be jealous. He was sorry that he had let Raven know that he intended to ask Yuka to be his mate.

Raven had also been hinting to Nauja that Yuka might be a bad choice because she was so head-strong. "You're

118   *h.c. Clarke*

going to have your hands full with that woman, Nauja," he said once. "If I were you, I would start now to curb her ways."

Another time, Raven had warned him, "People say Yuka might become as crazy as your mother because she is always talking to her in private. People should not be so private, Nauja. It is wrong. You should warn her. She is not making friends with the right people."

Nauja let these comments go, but he did not like the way Raven was behaving. *Where did my good friend go? This is not the Raven I grew up with. I don't understand his negativity. Has he changed, or was he always like this and I just didn't notice because he was so much nicer to me than the other boys? What was it Old Átenaq said, "Ravens are notorious for stealing and holding grudges?" Raven shouldn't have a grudge against me. I have done nothing.*

The last part of what Old Átenaq said popped into his head. "Nauja this is the most important of all, Ravens will attack the nest of sea going birds." *What could he have possibly meant by that?*

Old Átenaq insisted his grandson be offered a dog, but Raven refused. Raven claimed his duties kept him from giving the amount of time required to be trained. Nauja was relieved but felt Raven didn't want to take orders from him or clean up after a dog.

Raven seemed overly worried about his image. Nauja remembered Old Átenaq's words at the beginning of his trek, "The Raven is able to persuade stronger animals to do his work for him. Then steal the prize right out from under their noses."

Nauja tried teasing Raven the way he did Sacha, "You guessed who I am going to name as my mate. Will you tell me who you will be picking? Have you decided? Or is it that too many girls have lined up in front of you begging for the honor?"

"Who I pick is my business, Nauja. Just because you have gained greater status than you deserve, does not give you the right to analyze or even comment on my choice," Raven had snapped.

"What do you mean greater than I deserve, Raven? Is not my gift of dogs significant? Have they not established their worth?" Nauja challenged. It took all of his energy to resist an angry tone.

"They seem to be useful beasts. But they are not people. I brought back ten skilled hunters and ten skilled fishermen. They are all willing to become full members of our tribe. And this in just the minimum two moons, I might add. I was back before the first dark-moons. Beasts should not have awarded you the status of advisor. Be careful, my friend, you may not be as influential as you think you are," Raven snapped.

Nauja did not want to be contradictory but couldn't help but challenge this warning. "Raven, I do not think that I am powerful at all. I am just one tribe member among many. It is my philosophy that each person, male or female, is just as important as any other tribe member. Yes, we need hunters, but we need flint knappers as well. Where would hunters be without sharp spear points?

Raven sneered, "And in all likelihood that Yuka-woman has convinced you that she too is just as important as a hunter?"

Nauja checked his anger. "She did not have to convince me, Raven. I have held that belief all my life. Yes, women are just as important as men and not just because they bring forth the next generation. That is not their only function. In my perception, if a woman is strong and swift enough, she should be allowed to be a hunter herself."

"You will make many enemies with those radical ideologies, Nauja. Don't tell anyone else how you feel. I am your good friend. I understand that you and your father are under the spell of your mother. But others will not want you advising the chief with such strange beliefs."

Nauja walked away. He took Ktoh and went far away from the village. He needed to be alone. He wished he could have asked Yuka to come with him, but after the things Raven had said, Nauja thought it would not be wise to be seen walking out with her alone. He needed time to think, not about Yuka, but about Raven. The things Raven had said worried him.

The sun of the ceremony came. Each young man and each young woman dressed in their finest clothes. The young men were excited because they would first be accepted into the tribe as an adult. Then each, according to the value of his gift and the status it had awarded him, would name his choice of mate. The young woman would walk to the front to join her new mate. They would then go to the hut the families had built for them to start their new lives together.

Next came those who had not chosen a mate after a previous trek. Finally came still older men who wanted to replace a mate who had walked the wind. At the end came newcomers to the tribe. These were the men who had come with the trekkers. They would be initiated into the tribe. At that time, he could name a woman as a life partner.

This is when Sacha and the men who had followed Raven would step forward. Raven's followers would be first. Newcomers were awarded the status of the man who had brought them. Nauja looked around for Raven. Usually, they would stand together. But he couldn't find his friend.

The Ceremony began. Old Átenaq chanted the ancient words in a loud stately voice. Raven preceded everyone else, for he was Grandson-of-Chief. He walked to the front of the assembled crowd. Nauja noted that Raven would not look at him. This surprised Nauja. More of the ancient words were spoken and Raven was presented to the tribe as an adult.

Old Átenaq spoke again. "Raven, Son of my Son, have you chosen a woman to be your life partner? And if you have, state her name now that she may come forward and be recognized alongside of you and be celebrated by the tribe." The crowd listened intently. Raven had never shown a liking for any one young woman.

Raven turned to the community, and in a strong dynamic voice announced, "I choose Yuka as my mate that together we may face the journey of life."

Chapter 22

The Rift

I will be as cunning as a coyote.
Then I will prepare the way for my children and their children.

The whole community gasped.

The people had been eager to see which girl would be granted this greatest of all stations—to be chosen by an future chief. They had been listening intently to Raven's announcement, but no one had guessed that Yuka would be the one. The other young men farther down the line had been worried about their own choices, for no woman could possibly turn down the chance to be mate to a chief. Even though they were relieved that Raven had not chosen their women, they were still shocked.

Nauja stood in horror when he heard the loud, strong words of Raven. *How could he do that to me? He has always known my inclinations toward Yuka. He laughed at me for liking this outspoken girl who no one else would ever consider taking as mate. Just last fall he had said, "You should not have much competition there." All the scorn and warnings he has given me these past moons. Were they planned to make his choice more dramatic? He will tear her down, berate her, dominate her. He might even beat her. I can't let that happen. I can't let that happen.*

Before he could stop himself, Nauja stepped forward and shouted, "NO! Yuka is mine. She has always been mine. You do not want her. You only want her because I want her, and you are jealous of the status and influence I have gained."

In spite of the courage it took to cross the Grandson-of-Chief, the statement was credible. Everyone knew it. Raven was jealous of Nauja. Nauja had brought back something new. Raven had only gone the minimum two moons. His gift consisted of only new tribe members. And they did not have new skills. If he had not been Grandson-to-Chief, his gift would have lowered his status.

Raven was so jealous that he would yell at anyone who showed respect for Nauja. He had become angry when people said the dogs made life easier.

Raven, anger burning in his eyes, stepped forward and cried out, "You defy my right to state the woman of my choice, Nauja, son of Crazy-Woman? You dare to turn this sacred ceremony into chaos?

"Did you come back to benefit the tribe? Maybe you want to change it into a different tribe? How dare you upset the most important ceremony of our tribe. I contend that you are no longer a Beringian. You should not be allowed to join as a full adult member."

After an initial gasp, this statement stunned the people to silence. Even Old Átenaq didn't know what to do. Something like this had never happened before. And then the inconceivable happened. Ktoh raised her snout to the sun and howled. It was a long, warning howl. Each dog, wherever it was, answered her, lifting its snout to the sky and howled in return. Even Ata, who had never left the side of Old Átenaq since the sun he had been called forward by the old man, added his voice.

Old Átenaq put one hand to his chest. He reached the other toward Ata. Ata turned to the old man. The one brown and the one blue eye connected to the pain Átenaq's. The old man, for that's what he was, not a chief, just an old man in pain, slumped to the ground, still grasping Ata's fur in his hand.

The crowd gasped again. No one knew what to do. The current advisors rushed forward. But Ata showed his teeth, growling in such a threatening way that they did dare to approach closer.

"See what evil those beasts can do?" Kanik called out from the crowd. He still resented Nauja for having gotten the better of him the day the new pups were born. "Nauja has brought evil spirits among us. Nauja is to blame."

Yuka, Nunyae, and many other women came toward the old man. Amaak was blocked by the advisors. "You are mother to Nauja. You may not approach until a determination is made on the cause Chief Átenaq's death."

"Surely it is indisputable," screamed one of Kanik's friends.

"That's true," screamed one of Nauja's. "It is indisputable that Nauja is not guilty. Raven attacked Nauja. Nauja did nothing to Raven."

"What about interrupting the ceremony. Nauja was at fault there," came the response.

"That has nothing to do with Raven attacking Nauja."

"What about Dōshi's attack on the child? What about that?"

"Dōshi did not attack a child. He saved her. And besides that has nothing to do with this situa…"

"Now, now," shouted an elder. "We can see that there are diverse opinions. All will be decided in good time."

Ata allowed the women to approach and place Old Átenaq gently on a skin. The men carried him into the main lodge. Ata followed, guarding the lodge. Ata and his sharp teeth and growl decided who was allowed to enter and who was not.

People were screaming and shouting at Nauja, portraying him as evil, calling for his death or banishment. The whole tribe was involved. Some called for the death of Nauja and all the dogs, and some defending them. Old disputes between men were brought up that had nothing to do with what had happened.

The people separated into sides. Half the tribe stood behind Raven. They yelled across an empty space. The other half stood beside Nauja. They defended him and the dogs.

Raven stepped forward into the clearing between the groups. The people backed away giving him plenty of room. Raven shouted again in a bold aggressive voice, "I will be chief now, Nauja. My father walks with the wind. Old Átenaq is talking with the wind as we speak, and I am chief. I will have the mate I choose, and I will have Yuka. She cannot turn down the opportunity to be mate-of-chief. She is mine and you will leave this tribe for good and take all your evil beasts with you. I do not want them here. My people do not want them here. The old ways are good enough for us."

"The old chief lives!" cried a woman from the door of the main lodge. But no one heard her, least of all Raven.

Nauja looked at Raven with sadness. Where was the friendship they had had all their lives? Where was the Raven who had stood between him and the other bullying boys? Nauja bowed his head and spoke softly, "Raven, I will pledge my allegiance to you as I did to Old Átenaq before the long night. But you must let me have Yuka, and if you won't then at least allow her to choose. That is the only ethical thing to do."

"NO!" yelled Raven. "She will not choose. She will be mine, Mate-of-Chief. And she will learn to act like it. Her parents have let her become exceedingly self-important. She must learn to be a proper woman. She will not learn that with you. You have told me that yourself."

"She has a right to choose, Raven," Nauja countered quietly. "Every woman has a right to choose. We do not have slaves here. Women are not the property of their mates, they are partners. That is the way it has always been. If she consents to be your mate, I will stay silent. And if she wants me to leave the tribe, I will leave. Let her decide. I will accept her decision."

Raven's face turned red and bloated. He was angered by Nauja's calm wisdom. He could not contain his spite.

"She does NOT have the right to choose. Women are given to men by the chief. They are no more important than a good spear; less important even. And I am chief. You insult me, no you insult the tribe by saying a woman has a right to choose anything. From this sun forward, *I* will decide who joins with whom. That is the first policy I will pass." And he rushed forward pushing Nauja with all his might.

Nauja avoided Raven's first attack . He stepped away at the last moment. Raven became angrier. He was looking like a fool in front of the whole tribe. "You will pay for this Nauja," Raven roared. He moved to Nauja's right. When Nauja stepped left, as Raven knew he would, Raven charged. "You are so predictable

Only-Child-of-Crazy Woman," Raven sneered.

Raven never guessed that Nauja would stand up for himself. He had been so pitiful when he was young. Raven had defended him because it made Raven look like a better person. He had felt the same as the other boys. He had taken pleasure in watching the boys tease the weak son of the lowest tribesman.

When Raven charged, Nauja set his feet, tightened his belly into a rigid shield and put his forearms forward to block the young leader. Nauja's actions had been so unexpected, Raven lost his balance. He stumbled backwards and fell. He hit his head on a mammoth rib support of a hut. Everyone around heard the crack of his skull.

Nauja had done nothing to crack Raven's skull. But Raven was Grandson-of-Chief. And everyone also knew that Grandson-of-Chief must never lose at anything, must never be touched let alone shoved.

When Raven did not get up, Nauja looked around. What should he do? He had not killed Raven. All had seen it. He had not even pushed Raven. He had simply prepared his body to receive the blow. It had not been his fault.

The crowd surged and surrounded Nauja. Kanik's desire for revenge was not just an emotional reaction but a physical one as well. He and his supporters wanted blood. Nauja was puzzled. He had never seen his people so mad, so enraged.

Sacha grabbed Ktoh and dragged her to the pen behind Nauja's hut. He secured her tightly with several rawhide braids. Ktoh would die defending Nauja. Sacha must keep her safe until Nauja could get out of this trouble. Nunyae, three-month-old Chahká strapped to her back, said, "I will stay with both dogs until you come to get us.

"Go, Sacha. Go back to the gathering area. Try to help Nauja, but remember you are a stranger. Be careful. You must appear neutral. Nauja has made both friends and enemies this season. We must unify his friends without transmitting our intentions to his enemies."

Sacha returned to the crowd. *A revolution is beginning. Nauja is just a symbol of the disappointments in the lives of his enemies.*

Chapter 23
The Plan
**We cannot discover new oceans,
unless we have the courage to lose sight of the shore.**

Sacha found that Nauja had been taken away, his wrists and ankles bound with strong sinews, so Sacha backed away quietly. He had to think. *As a newcomer I cannot advocate for him; I would not be believed. Consequently, we have only one option; we must leave the tribe, and we must do it tonight.*

He returned to Yuka, Treenat, Ktoh and Dōshi. Nunyae, Miru and Nauja's parents were there too. Quiet Oomsa was standing behind Yuka, off to one side.

"I wouldn't have accepted," Yuka declared. It would have been a shameful embarrassment for Raven, but I wouldn't have accepted. I couldn't have. And he knew that. That's why he couldn't allow me to choose. Now what will happen, Sacha? What will they do to Nauja?"

"Do not say anything more, Yuka. And Nunyae, you too stay clear of everyone. Stay in Amaak's hut tonight, all of you. Stay unseen. I will creep about and find out what is happening.

When the twilight comes, each of you pack a sledge for a long trip. Pack it full of dried meat, skins, and tools. But take only necessary things. Nauja will not be welcome now, and I will not stay if he leaves. Amaak and Tukkuk, you must come with us. You will no longer be welcome either and no one will be here to protect you."

"Where will we go?" Amaak inquired? Will we go back to your tribe? Will we go back to Nunyae's tribe?"

"No, we will go east. We will immigrate to a new land and start a new tribe."

"East?" Amaak gasped. "There *is* no east. The Great Ice Wall marks the end of the world. There is nothing past the wall and the storms of sand that come from them. Only the great animals come from the wall."

"That can't be true, Amaak. I come from farther south. My

people could not see to the east. Instead of a wall of ice, we had an endless sea. But they entered the sea and risked their lives. They found the islands where I come from. And we have lived there as long as anyone in my tribe can remember. There are many legends and songs that tell us we did not stop on the islands. Only some of us did.

"The songs say that others got back in their boats and continued east. Their boats were sound and waterproof. The stories say that the boats dragged other boats behind filled with food and sealed containers of water. No one ever came back, so no one knows, but we accept that the eastern sea is not the end. Every so often a group of young people builds boats like those in the stories and sets out. These young people have never returned in defeat nor has any washed ashore drowned.

"We will go east. We will follow the caribou and the mammoth who go east. They would not be going into nothingness. We will follow the mammoth and go east."

"What about me, Sacha? What should I do?" demanded Miru.

"Miru, you must choose. Will you go with us to lands unseen, or will you stay to return to your own tribe? The choice has to be yours and yours alone," responded Sacha.

Miru remained quiet for a few moments. "I will go with you. Nunyae is of my tribe, so I will not be completely alone. The elders knew I might not come back. I want to go with you and Nauja. I want to see lands unknown."

"None of us will be alone, Miru," Sacha answered. We will all be strangers in a strange land."

With the decision made, Sacha crept back to the main lodge area. He kept to himself behind the huts. In the cleared space before the main lodge, groups had formed. Sacha could hear the shouting and arguing. The people had taken sides. The tribe was divided.

Old Átenaq lived, but Nauja was being blamed for Raven's death. When Old Átenaq decided to walk the wind, who would take his place as leader? It was always assumed that Raven would be there to take his place, to lead the tribe, to make the hard decisions. Now who would do that?

There was no one left in Old Átenaq's line. Kanik, the

grandson of Átenaq's brother, was taking the lead. His status had just improved beyond his wildest dreams. And he was taking advantage of it. He tried to hide his new desire and pretend sadness and insult on behalf of his cousin. He not only wanted Nauja killed, he wanted him killed in a horrible way.

"We should break his arms and legs and drag him out to the tundra and leave him to be eaten alive by the wolves he seems to love so much. Let's see if the beasts bow to him then, huh? Let's see if he becomes their leader or their meal," Kanik shrieked. His new power and outrageous ideas made those who would conflict with him scared to express their dissent.

"Yes, let's break his limbs and leave him for the wolves and the bears. Break the legs of the beasts he brought with him too. Leave them all out for vultures and the other carrion eaters," they cried.

At this, the handlers of the dogs as well as the handlers of the pups still in training slunk back to their outer huts, harnessed their dogs and brought them to Amaak's and Tukkuk's hut. They didn't know where else to go. Tukkuk was sitting guard while the women prepared for the journey inside. Sacha had told them to keep their preparations a secret.

When the dog handlers came to his hut, Tukkuk talked with them. None wanted to give up his dog. All were willing to leave the tribe with their families. Tukkuk hid the dogs inside the new hut he and Nauja had built for Nauja's new family. Each handler told his dog to be silent and then returned to his own hut to prepare for a long journey. They were to meet again at Tukkuk's hut when the moon was full. They would drag their own sledges packed and ready and bring their families.

Back at the main lodge, Sacha hid at the edge of the crowd listening in horror to the angry shrieks of the crowd. Some defended Nauja. Some even wanted Nauja to be chief. But fear usually overtakes reason, and the anger of the crowd grew. It was late into the night now. Those with reason tried to hold the hysteria at bay. But it did no good.

A woman came from the main lodge and tried to shout above the crowd. Old Átenaq was awake. Ata was still by his side exercising his own authority. Átenaq remembered what had happened. When he was told of Raven's death, tears ran down his cheeks. He called for Nauja, but no one would tell him where Nauja was or the death he was facing.

Sacha listened until he found out where Nauja was being kept. Oomsa appeared from the shadows. Sacha had never heard her speak before, but now she spoke with quiet authority. "Go back to the others, Sacha. They need you to organize them, and you will be recognized as Nauja's second. No one ever pays attention to me. I will go to free Nauja, but all must be ready to leave the moment we appear."

"But Oomsa, your parents are on Kanik's side and want to see Nauja and the dogs killed. Are you truly going against your parents, or are you trying to trick me? Not that you would tell me if you were," Sacha added, doubt filling his voice.

"I am going against my parents as I have done all my life when they tried to keep me away from Yuka. Go. Get everyone ready. I'm going to free Nauja." And with that she disappeared, blending into her surroundings as she always did.

She crept to the back of the hut where Nauja lay, bound and quiet. Nauja was lying in a low hut, wrists and ankles tied, staring up at the skins covering the mammoth ribs which formed the Beringian huts. He was waiting to hear his fate. He would probably be killed in the early sun. Banishment was too good for the killer of Grandson-of-Chief. He just hoped his death would be a quick one.

Chapter 24
Flight
When doubt no longer exists for you, then go forward with courage.

"Pssst, Nauja. Are you awake?"

"Who is there? Sacha, is that you? What are you doing here? You will join in my punishment if you speak to me."

"No, it's Oomsa. I've come to free you."

"Go away. I will not have another death on my soul."

"And I will not have the death of my leader on *my* soul," Oomsa replied. She had slit the hides in back of the hut and had entered it. "Lie still while I cut your ties. You cannot travel far secretly if you spill your blood on the ground. We are leaving. Sacha is organizing everyone right now. Beaver and Fiery Sky as well as the rest of the handlers and their families are going with us. We will travel far and start our own tribe. Quick, get up. We have to go."

They slipped out through the cut Oomsa had made at the back of the hut and crept behind the others, staying away from the light of hearth fires. When they reached the hut of Nauja's parents there were over two hands of extended families waiting, ready to leave. The handlers had quietly retrieved others from the crowd they knew would want to leave.

Each family had packed a sledge filled with provisions and tools. The sledges were fashioned in the old way to be dragged by one branch. *I will teach them the new halter I devised when there is time,* Nauja thought.

Nauja spoke to the handlers first, "Is any of you willing to give up your dog? Chief still lives and I do not want him to be without the use of dogs. The tribe will come to its senses under Old Átenaq's leadership. We will not leave any with eyes that do not match."

They did not have to decide. There were only three full-grown females that had matching eyes. Each dog was tethered, and the handlers left, unable to hide the tears that escaped down their cheeks. They had truly grown to love their dogs, but their new leader had asked them for this sacrifice, so they were willing to part with their dogs.

As quietly as possible with such a large group, they stole out of the community and headed east. Sacha assured them it would be all right to go east. They walked all night, both dogs and men dragging sledges, boys and women bending to heavy knapsacks or babies on their backs in the old way. Even the smaller children were dragging or carrying items according to their size.

When the sun's first pink rays came over the mountains, Sacha turned to his friend. "We must turn directly south here. No more than an hour's walk. I have a surprise to show you."

"Would this have anything to do with your disappearances these past moons?," prodded Nauja.

Sacha smiled his gap-toothed grin, "Yes. At the time I was building them, I thought they would be my manhood gift to my new tribe as is your tradition. Now we will use them to betray it," sighed Sacha. The band of people turned south and by the time the pink had disappeared from the sky, they arrived at the sea.

Sacha led Nauja to three huge piles of brush and scrub birch on the rock beach just above the water's edge. He removed the brush and branches revealing three structures covered in thick skins sewn tightly together and heavily oiled. "These are boats in the style of my people but adapted for this northern climate by using skins from sea mammals. If these sea mammals do not get wet, neither will we."[i]

"Sacha, you are not saying that we take them with us? How will we carry them?" Nauja stammered, unsure of how to react.

"We will be followed, Nauja. The Tribe cannot afford to lose this many hunters. I had meant to show you how to fish the big sea whales. I saw them not far out when we first arrived. Now we will use my boats to escape. But my boats are few and cannot carry our entire group. We have to split

---

[i] Genetic studies of modern Steller's sea lions suggest that this sea mammal likely sunned out on the rocks along Beringia's south shore. Migrants may have had their pick of seafaring mammals.

h.c. Clarke

up. The Tribe cannot follow both groups. I will take half by sea following the coast while you walk the others east through the mountains and then south. My band will find a good site along the sea and south of the ice mountain. We will wait for you. Do not worry, Ktoh will find Dōshi."

Nauja objected, "No! We cannot separate. We are one tribe, a new tribe. We are stronger together, Sacha. Breaking up would make us weaker and leave us vulnerable to capture should the Beringians catch up to us."

"You know I'm right, Nauja," Sacha argued. "Think about it. It is the logical move. Beringian hunters cannot follow both of us. We will wait for you on the coast beyond the ice sheet. Ktoh will find Dōshi."

"Let me take a moment, Sacha," Nauja replied and turned his head to hide the tear threatening to escape his left eye to make its way down his face. "Let me take just a moment to think." Nauja turned suddenly and headed away from the group to be alone.

Once alone, he stood silently, looking up to the blue star, and begged for help in making this decision. "Blue Star give me help; I'm begging you. It was my fault all these people have left their homes. I am now responsible for their welfare.

"I turned Sacha away from the traditions of his home so that he felt he could not return. He, then, chose Nunyae and took her from the comfort of her ancestors. Then I challenged a future leader for the woman I loved which ended in his death. I am not old enough or wise enough to make these decisions alone.

"Please help me Blue Star. You came to me as a child guiding me to find Ktoh. You gave me the vision of the earthquake. Give me a vision now. Help me."

The Blue Star answered him, speaking directly to him this one time, "You are resourceful, Nauja, the Seagull. As your name indicates, you can adapt to many climates.

Take the girl Yuka, the Bright Star, and those who would follow you and head into the wind to the east. When you cannot go any further, keep me at your back and let your wings carry you over the land.

Your dear friend, Sacha, must take his group by boat and follow the coast. Your children and their children and their children will cover the land and be happy as long as you do three things for me."

"Anything Blue Star. I wish only that my people be happy and healthy," replied Nauja.

Then the star warned, "The first, and most important, of my rules is that you must always respect the land you are on and take care of it. Place its welfare above all else in the world. The land will give you what you need.

The second thing I require is that you take care of each other. Whether you are near or far, treat each person as your brother or sister. The third thing I request of you is to name a child Seagull or Star skipping no more than one generation, but, and this is the hardest part of my third request, you must let the Star and the Seagull fly away from you when they are ready. They will start new tribes as you are now doing, and they will spread my three laws across this beautiful land that I am giving you."

"Yes, Blue Star. I will always follow your three laws. I give you my word." Nauja returned to the little band he had led to this place. "Sacha, I have received advice from the Blue Star. I am to let you go your way and hope that we meet to the south."

Nauja put his hands-on Sacha's upper arms, "I started my journey two sun cycles past, filled with fear, filled with doubt, a lowly born, unimportant son of the tribe. But first I met Ktoh, and then I met you. It turned out to be the best two cycles of my life. Now I am the leader of a tribe of my own. I wish I could say you are wrong, but I can't.

"The Blue Star spoke to me. It told me two important things. It told me that I and those who follow me must worship the land. 'Take care of the land,' the Blue Star said, 'and it will take care of the people.' And then it told me the saddest thing of all, that when the time comes, we have to let go of those we love.

h.c. Clarke

And so, Sacha, I must let you go and trust that we will find each other again in a place where the land will take care of us all. I want you to know that you are, and always will be, my brother. Just in case our meeting is in the stars, Sacha, take another of the dual eyed females with you."

Sacha also became emotional, "My journey has been just like yours. I left to explore the world to see what was across the sea, over the mountains. And what I found was a brother and a mate. We will meet again, my brother. Be sure of that. We *will* meet again. Ktoh will find Dōshi."

Delayed goodbyes were not possible; the sun was progressing. Sacha was directing his group on how to balance the boats, who must be in the front and who must be in the back, and how to work the paddles. Those continuing by foot, tears on their cheeks, bent their heads into the eastern winds and headed for the ice mountains to the east.

A blue star shone in the sky. A blue star that did not move. The walkers headed east, the star at their left. The boaters headed south, the star at their backs. Neither group knew what lay ahead. But they both had a goal, move south, establish a new tribe, find a new life; beyond the ice.

Chapter 25
The Star and the Seagull
It takes a thousand voices to tell a single story.

In the centuries that followed, the story of Nauja, Yuka, and Ktoh became a legend. It was passed on from generation to generation. As groups broke away from the mother nation, the legend was repeated. Soon all the people on the north and south continents of the land given to the Dog Star People retold the story in some form.

The Star and the Seagull[i]

In the time when all birds lived as one, there was a fledgling Seagull who was timid and withdrawn. The other young birds pecked at him mercilessly. The Raven stood back and watched the others with a gleam in his eye. When Raven thought the young seagull had had enough, he stepped in and stopped the others. "I am your friend, Seagull. I will protect you."

Seagull did not feel protected, and he did not see friendship in Raven's eyes, but none of the other birds had offered friendship, so he did Raven's bidding and thought he was loved.

One evening the seagull looked up in the sky and saw a small, bright star. The small star shone brighter so that the Seagull could approach her.

"Why do you shine so brightly, small star?" he asked her.

"Should I not shine to the best of my ability?" she asked. "Should I shine less just because I am small?"

"You are right, Bright Star. You should shine as you feel you can. No one should tell you to shine less because of your size."

The seagull fell in love with the small bright star that dared to shine her best. The star also fell in love. She had never met anyone who understood her right to shine according to her abilities.

---

[i] This legend is the creation of the author and is not embodied in any Native American or First Nation culture.

h.c. Clarke

"Join with me in ceremony, Bright Star," cried the seagull. "I want to face the future with you at my side."

"I want the same," replied the bright little star. "Fly to me. If you can reach me, we will face the future together.

The seagull tried his best to fly to the star, but he could not reach her. Every evening as soon as he saw the bright little star, he gathered his energy and flew with all his strength toward her. And each night, the Bright Star gathered her own energy and shone brighter, so the seagull could keep trying long after the sun had set. Still the seagull could not reach her.

The other young birds made fun of him. "HAH," replied the Raven. "That star shines beyond her station. A small star like her should stay in her place. She has no right to shine so brightly."

The next night the bright little star spoke to him, "Go," she advised. "Go and find yourself. Find your strength. It is there inside you. Then you shall be able to reach me."

So young Seagull left to find his strength. When he returned some did not like his newly found strength. Raven became jealous of Seagull's competence and the influence he seemed to have over others. Raven's anger and jealousy had blinded his judgement, and he flew head-first into a large tree and fell dead on the ground. Seagull knew he must leave. He flew into the sky searching for Bright Star. There she was shining brighter and brighter. Seagull flew higher and higher until he could fly no more. Just as he was about to plummet to his death, the Star-That-Does-Not-Move spoke to the couple.

"Seagull, Bright Star!" he called to the lovers. "Your persistence and courage deserve reward. I have decided the two of you should be together. I will change you into new beings so you may face the future side by side. As long as you follow three simple rules, you may be together."

"First you must take care of the land on which you live. As long as you take care of the land, it will provide you with everything you need to thrive. Next you must take care of each other and those who follow you. Life would be meaningless without loved ones. Finally, you must name a child Seagull or Star," continued the Star-That-Does-Not-Move. "By doing so, you will be honoring your heritage. But should your children want to spread their wings and fly away, you must let them. This way, your children will teach my rules across the land."

The Star-That-Does-Not-Move spoke one last time, "I am also giving you a gift. Of all the animals in the world, there is one that has no special ability. She is not fierce like Wolf, nor is she shrewd like Coyote. She does not have sharp claws like Cougar, nor does she have the size of Bear. But Dog has something no other animal has. She has love and loyalty. I am giving you Dog; she will follow you anywhere, comfort you in grief, and defend your life above her own. She will remind you of her traits that you may admire and pursue them as your own.

"Dog will help you and teach you. Most of the time Dog will follow, but sometimes you must let her lead. The dog I am giving you is special among her kind. Her eyes are of two colors, one brown that keeps her on the earth and one blue that allows her to focus on the sky. Keep one of her kind near you at all times and she will help you care for the other animals."

And so, the small bright star and the devoted seagull were changed into human beings filled with the energy, optimism, and courage of youth. They joined in ceremony and faced the future together, side-by-side as equal partners.

When their human lives were over, Seagull and Bright Star were sent into the sky together. There they shine with equal brightness as they watch over their progeny below. They were known as Chamukuy, the bird, but are now called Theta and Tauri in the constellation of Taurus.

The Star-That-Does-Not-Move sent the dog with the two-colored eyes into the sky as well. Her name is Sirius. She too is a twin star system. She and her mate can be found in the constellation of Canis Major, and, of all the stars in the night sky, shine the brightest. Chamukuy and Canis Major are two of the five brightest constellations in the sky.

Sometimes nations break up due to strife as in Nauja's experience, and sometimes they spread due to curiosity as in Sacha's tribe. Sometimes division is expected, a built-in part of the culture.

h.c. Clarke

The first humans on the North American continent may have come over the land through an ice-free corridor, following the route Nauja took, they may have come by boat along the coast as Sacha did, or they may have sailed from island to island as the stories Sacha's people tell. They may have come by all three methods. We do not know.

Whatever the reason, whatever the method, people moved from Siberia or Asia onto the North American continent. Their offspring dispersed and populated over the 9.5 million square miles of North America and the 6.8 million square miles of South America. When the great ice sheets melted, the land called Beringia was flooded and is now under 300 feet of water, and the coast lines are farther inland than they were. For these reasons archeological sites are few making the mystery of how we got here almost unsolvable.

About the author

Ms. Clarke was a teacher for 41 years in grades K-12, community college, and as a teacher of English in Mexico. Her favorite age level is middle school where she spent her last eleven years in Central Point, Oregon teaching English to students who spoke a language other than English at home.

She received her undergraduate degree in Elementary Education from Syracuse University and her master's degree in Curriculum Development from Boston University. She also studied at the University of Rennes, France and El Instituto Cultural de Oaxaca, Mexico.

Ms. Clarke was born and raised in a Chicago suburb. The twelve acres of woods next to her house provided her with abundant opportunities in which to create different worlds. During her teen years, she spent many Saturdays at The Field Museum of Natural History and The Brookfield Zoo, always alone so she could stay at an exhibit for as long as she wanted. Much of the time she observed the people looking at the exhibits as much as the exhibits themselves.

Books by h.c. Clarke

Beyond the Ice. Nauja takes most of his followers through the ice-free corridor until it ends. Sacha takes some in boats on the open seas along the coast. Will they meet again. What adventures do each of them have on their trip below the ice sheet? And does Ktoh find Dōshi?

The Yellow Seagull—Walks While Talking, a young boy from the Great Plains who is on the autistic spectrum, is put in charge of a group travelling across the vast North American Continent to meet the yellow Seagull in a place where the great salty waters never end. Mafúr, a boy from the Norse Viking culture leaves his home to find the Blue Star of his destiny, a girl from the Dorsett culture on Baffin Island. Will they get there in time? Will Mafúr's kin follow him when they escape to the land with trees that touch the sky?

Coming Soon

Battle of Spirits—Kwani is the son of a slave and is living at the mouth of what is now the Columbia River in Washington State. He has a vision of a star-woman who awaits his arrival beneath a bleeding mountain. Although Kwani is reluctant to go, the shaman of his tribe sends him to find the world where the sky is falling and the star-woman awaits him.

Finding Home, The Early Colonies 1586-1635—In a two-generational story, Gaviota is the 12-year-old son of a Conquistador and a Timucua woman in San Agustín, FL. His adventures include being kidnapped by the colonists at Roanoke as well as by a British pirate. The second half of the book is about his son, Larus, at the colonies of Jamestown and Plymouth and finally the founding of Providence, Rhode Island.

Yasi and Stella, A Story of The Industrial Revolution—Yasi is the son of a wealthy factory owner; Stella is the daughter of an Irish immigrant. There is a mystery surrounding Yasi's birth, and he must find out how he fits into the world around him. Stella's life is in the woolen mill, but she is an inventor in her mind. How can she make people see that women understand machines?

GLOSSARY

Word	Synonym	Word	Synonym
according to	as said by	aspects	features, sides
accordingly	so, therefore	assemble	gather, collect
accuracy	precision	assertion	statement, claim
accurately	exactly	assertive/ly	self-confident, firm
acquire	obtain, get	assume	suppose
additional	extra,	assumptions	guesses
adequate/ly	enough	authentic	genuine, real
administrate	manage, govern	authenticity	genuineness
advocate	sponsor	authority	expert, power
affect (v)	change	availability	obtainability
allocate/ion	assign	basically	essentially
alternative	substitute	capacity	volume, size
amend	modify, change	capture	take, seize
analysis	study	characteristic[(adj)]	trait, feature
analytically	logically	clarification	clearing up
analyze	examine	clearly	obviously, plainly
anticipation	eagerness	code	system, policy
appeal	plea, attract	coherent	clear, articulate
applicable	relevant	collaborate	work together
approach	come near	collapse	fall down
appropriately	suitably	commodity	product, goods
approximate	estimated, near	common/ly	everyday
articulate [(adj)]	expressive	comparable	equal, like
articulate [(v)]	speak clearly	competent	capable, able

Word	Synonym	Word	Synonym
compilation	composing,	convert	win over
compile	collect, gather	convey	express
complex/ity	difficult	convince	sway, convert
complicate	make difficult	correlate	associate, link
conceivable	possible, credible	correlation	connection
conclude	finish	credibility	trustworthy
concur	agree	credible	reliable
concurrent	at the same time	criteria	conditions
conflict (n)	argument	debatable	arguable
conflict (v)	disagree	debate	dispute
consent	agree, concur	decline	refuse
consequently	so, therefore	define	describe
considerably	noticeably	demonstrate	show
consideration	thought	depict/ion	show
consist	contain	design	drawing, scheme
consist of	be made of	despite	even though
constitutes	set up, creates	detect	find, identify
consult	ask, discuss	determination	resolve
consultation	meeting	determined	resolute
contend	declare, argue	development	progress
context	setting	devise	plan, formulate
contradictory	inconsistent	differentiate	tell apart
contribute	say, donate	diminish	reduce
contribution	role, say	discriminate	show prejudice
converse	talk with	disputable	debatable

distinct   inapplicable

Word	Synonym	Word	Synonym
distinct	different	exercise (v)	train, use
diverse	varied, assorted	exhibit/ion	display, show
document	text, record	expand	enlarge
domestic	local, family	exploit	abuse, misuse
dominate	control, rule	extended	stretch out, expanded
draft (v)	recruit	extent	amount, range
due to	because of	factor	feature, element
dynamic	lively, change	feature	trait, characteristic
economy	thrift, saving	federal	national
elaborate	intricate	focal	central
eligible	available	function	purpose, operate
emphasis	stress, weight	fundamental/ly	important, major
emphasize	call attention to	generally	normally, as a rule
employ	hire, use	generate	make create
equate	liken, link	genuine	honest, real
equip	prepare, supply	guarantee	promise
equipment	gear, tools	identify	recognize
essentially	basically	ideology	philosophy
evident/ly	apparently	illustrate	show
exaggerate	overstate	immigrate	move to
exceedingly	very, especially	impact	influence, affect
exclude	reject, leave out	imply	suggest
exclusive	select, private	inadequate/ly	insufficient
exercise (n)	use, practice	inapplicable	irrelevant

Word	Synonym	Word	Synonym
incentive	motivation	literal/ly	actual, exact
inclined/ation	leaning	locate	find
included	incorporated	maintain	keep, uphold
incoherent	rambling	major	main, foremost
inconceivable	beyond belief	marginal	bordering,
incorporate	integrate, include	maturity	experience, wisdom
indicate	point out	method	process
indicative of	suggestive of	modify	change, amend
indisputable	certain	motive	reason, purpose
individual	distinct	negative	bad, refusal
influence	power, sway	negativity	disapproval
influential	powerful	neutral	impartial
infrastructure	set-up	notorious	infamous
initial	original, mark	objective	neutral, goal
inquire	ask, find out	obvious/ly	clearly
integrate	mix, combine	participate	join, take part
intense	strong, deep	perception	view, opinion
internal	inner	period	era, stage
interpret	translate, clarify	periodically	regularly
invariably	always	phase	period, segment
isolate	separate, cut off	philosophy	values, beliefs
justify	defend, excuse	plausible	believable
labor	work, effort	policy	rule, program
legislate	authorize	portray	depict, describe
likelihood	probability	potential/ly	possible/ly

Word	Synonym	Word	Synonym
precede	go before	site	place, spot
precise	exact	specify	identify
preclude	prevent, stop	speculate	wonder, think
predominant	main, major	status	rank, position
presume	assume, suppose	strategic/ally	tactical, planned
prevent	block, stop	structure	building, make-up
previous	preceding, prior	subjective	one-sided
productive	useful	subsequently	then, next
prohibit	forbid, ban	subtle	delicate, faint
prompt (v)	incite, inspire	sufficient/ly	enough
prospect/ive	viewpoint	susceptible	vulnerable
purchase	buy, grasp	symbol	sign, image
radical	extreme	technology	skill, knowledge
recollection	memory	thereby	thus, so
relate	tell, connect	tradition	custom
relate	tell, connect	tradition	custom
require	force, insist on	transmit	convey, spread
restrict	limit	validity	soundness
resulting	bring about	vary/varied	differ, assorted
reveal	tell, show	virtual/ly	almost
revolution	rebellion, revolt	welfare	health, well-being
rigid	stiff, unbending		
secure	safe, protected		

Made in the USA
Middletown, DE
09 April 2024

52707774R00094